ONE WEEK WITH YOU

JR JENNER

Copyright © 2022 by JR Jenner.

The right of JR Jenner to be identified as the author of this work has been asserted in accordance with the Copyright, Designs and Patents Act 1988.

All rights reserved.

No part of this book may be reproduced in any form or by any electronic or mechanical means, including information storage and retrieval systems, without the permission of the copyright owner except for the use of brief quotations in a book review.

This story is a work of fiction. Names, characters, places, and incidents are either the products of the author's imagination or are used fictitiously. Any resemblance to actual events or persons, living or dead, is coincidental.

ASIN: B0BD95LPYK

Print ISBN: 9798358966949

Cover design: Haya in Designs.

Cover image: Jacob Lund/Shutterstock.com

Editing: Aimee Walker Editorial Services.

❦ Created with Vellum

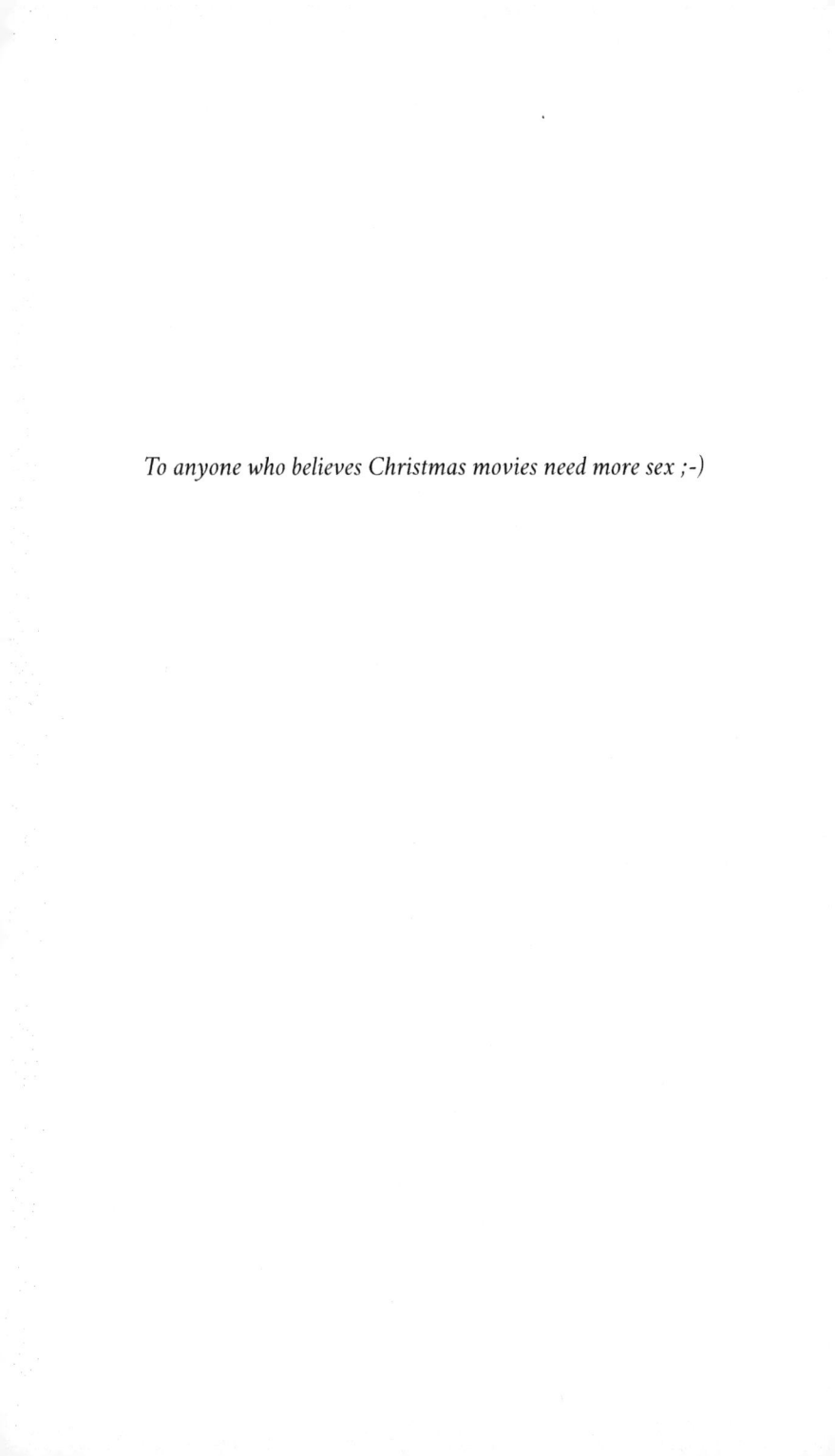

To anyone who believes Christmas movies need more sex ;-)

CONTENTS

Content Warning	vii
Chapter 1	1
Chapter 2	10
Chapter 3	19
Chapter 4	36
Chapter 5	58
Chapter 6	69
Chapter 7	80
Chapter 8	90
Chapter 9	102
Chapter 10	111
Chapter 11	122
Epilogue	135
What's next?	145
Dearest Reader	147
Acknowledgments	149
About the Author	151

CONTENT WARNING

This story contains strong language and explicit sexual content, brief discussions about absentee parents and references to a character being childless and wanting a baby.

CHAPTER 1

TALIA

This can't be happening.

"You're firing me?" I asked out loud this time, just to make sure. Despite the panicky chorus of *what the actual fuck* circling my brain, I sounded surprisingly calm. Collected, even. How, I didn't know.

My boss – ex-boss – Nadia looked up from her laptop without a care in the world or a facial expression and said, "That's what I said," before going back to whatever she was typing. Probably notes for her weekly presentation at Assholes Anonymous. Though, frankly, that was an insult to assholes.

She squinted at the screen like I no longer existed, and that careless dismissal, though nothing new, made me wonder why I'd put up with her all these years. The thought passed pretty quickly. The sad truth was, well, it had been my job. I had to admit I'd learned from her too. Not that I'd ever tell her that. It obviously helped that I earned good money doing something I enjoyed and was actually good at. I'd taken years to figure that out, jumping from one crappy career to the next. An asshole boss was nothing in comparison to what I'd gained, and compromises had to be made somewhere. But this…

This can't be happening!

Not now.

I'd just bought a flat. I had a mortgage. That first step onto the overpriced London property ladder had been shaky enough at my age, and that was with a well-paid job to support such a move. What the hell was I going to do now? No one hired this late in the year, least of all PR firms, and I wasn't cut out for a seasonal temp job in retail. Festive shoppers were scary enough to turn even my sunshine heart to stone. I still had scars from working at Topshop when I was seventeen. Actual, physical scars.

I have savings. I have savings. Not much, but it was something. They wouldn't last long though. Money never did. And then there was Christmas and…

I blinked, barely able to move, pulse pounding in my ears. Dread settled solidly in my throat. I'd be swallowing around that for weeks. "You're firing me less than a month before Christmas?"

If sighs could talk Nadia's sounded like *oh, she's still here*. "Yes, unfortunately. You understand it can't be helped."

"Uh, no?" A shrill, almost hysterical, sound bubbled up in my throat. "No, I don't understand. Two months ago there was talk about making me a partner in the new year. What changed?"

"What worked yesterday doesn't always work today, Talia. We're restructuring. Shaking things up. That's the name of the PR game. You know we have to keep things…" She paused to look me up and down. "Fresh."

Ah. In other words, they had to keep things *young*. Got it. Loud and clear. Rage forced my fingernails into the flesh of my palms.

"I'm sorry, but it had to be done," Nadia continued, as if

she hadn't just punched me in the heart. With a brick. She picked up a collection of files on her desk and shuffled them with a definitive tap that might as well have been *the end*. "Now, I think it's best if you leave the office quietly. You don't want to be the person who makes a scene, do you?"

I huffed out a bitter laugh, not even the slightest bit amused. "Oh, the horror," I said and walked away, head held high despite the sting of tears.

One thing I'd learned was to never let them see me cry.

In all my years working at NT Public Relations I had accumulated surprisingly few personal items, which turned out to be a blessing as I left the building for the last time. I didn't even need the repurposed file box my friend Ellie had pilfered from office supplies before I did the walk of shame back through the office, desperately trying to ignore the whispers of shock.

Everything personal I'd previously stashed on my desk – a framed photo of myself and my three brothers, a selection of red and pink lipsticks, a pair of French Sole ballet flats, and a mystery novel I'd been trying to read on my lunch break for six years – fit into my oversized shoulder bag with room to spare.

Ten years and it was like I'd never been there at all. The thought sat uncomfortably in the pit of my stomach. A blistering rage burned the back of my throat, like I'd swallowed a jar of nails. I needed to scream into a pillow as soon as possible. Maybe smash a few plates, not that I'd ever done that sort of thing. But there was a first time for everything.

I willed myself to move forward. No looking back. Stomping along the street, I tightened my coat against the December chill and glared at all the Christmas displays in shop windows. Mini trees and snowflake decals, pine cones and twinkling lights. All these cute festive things usually drew a smile to my lips and joy to my heart, but now I didn't know how to feel anything but angry, and overwhelmed.

Blindsided.

I thought back to the me of this morning, mere hours ago, bouncing into the office with a tray of coffees for my team. I'd had absolutely no idea. How could I have been so clueless? That wasn't me. Anticipating what was coming next was part of my damn job.

Maybe I deserved to get the sack.

A flash of lightning lit the dark grey sky above, followed by a low rumble of thunder. Perfect mood-matching weather. I scowled but picked up the pace a bit. My shadow disappeared as I reached the Thames Embankment ten minutes later and fat drops of rain scattered at my feet, stabbing at my cheeks and eyes like icy needles. Within seconds I was drenched, the moisture flattening my blonde hair enough that it probably looked brown.

"Really?" I shouted and gestured helplessly at the sky, giving an angry cloud the middle finger before running for the cover of a nearby tree. "Why couldn't we have snow instead? It's fucking December. Act like it for once!"

An elderly lady paused to give me a weird, startled look from beneath her umbrella and all I could manage was a shrug. "It's been a day, sorry!" I called after her.

I must've looked like a wreck.

I couldn't stop shivering as I wiped at the mascara smudged under my eyes and wrung out my hair, fingers like shards of ice. All the while, the rain poured down in sheets and gathered in puddles. Sniffling, I shook my head and laughed. Sniffled again. Laughed once more. It seemed silly but there was no other option. If I didn't laugh, I'd cry, and I tried so hard not to do that. I believed in the power of smiles and laughter, even when life didn't give me reasons for either of them.

I tried anyway.

My phone chose that moment to ring, and I dug into the depths of my bag with a sigh, swearing under my breath at the name lighting up the screen. For a split second, I considered letting it go to voicemail, and for another split-second felt bad about it. Instead, I fixed my face with a smile no one would see, but it took three swipes of my wet fingers against the touchscreen to answer.

"Hi, Mum!" I said with fake brightness.

"Hi, honey," she replied, and I had to bite back my irritation at her perky tone. It wasn't her fault I was having a bad day. "Just calling to remind you about lunch on Sunday. I'm doing a roast, and I'll make the potatoes extra crispy if you promise not to be late."

"I'll be there, I promise. 1 p.m., wasn't it?"

"Oh! No last-minute PR disaster you have to clean up?"

I rolled my eyes. Okay, so I'd been known to miss a dinner or two for work and Joanna Johnson, gold medallist of guilt trips, was never going to let me forget it.

"Not this time," I admitted. My stomach dropped at the reminder of my unexpected unemployment, and I wondered how long I'd be feeling that punch of absolute terror. "I'm all yours."

"Wonderful. We can't wait to see you. And this means we can finally talk about Christmas!"

"Can we not?" I groaned, not least because our Christmas plans never really changed year after year. But the thought of festive drinks with friends, as well as the numerous family get-togethers that usually filled my December calendar, now filled me with horror. There was nothing worse than telling people you hadn't seen in a year that your life had gotten worse. What would I even say? *Hi, how are you? Oh, me? Just got fired and now might lose my home, but it's fine. No worries at all! Merry Christmas and a Happy New Year!*

Absolutely fucking not.

"It's December already!" Mum whined. "You still haven't emailed your gift list."

"You don't check your emails."

"Then send me a text."

I scrubbed at my forehead, closing my eyes. It took everything in me not to sigh out loud. "You don't know how to open your messages."

"Well, you need to tell me somehow! What do your brothers want? And Rafe? I'm sure he'll be spending the day with us again, and I never know what to get him. What do you buy for a man who has everything?"

The mention of Rafe set my pulse flaring, though it wasn't exactly a new sensation. My heart had been lighting up that way for years. I should probably be used to it, except I wasn't. Not at all. But that was a problem for another day.

"You ask me the same thing every year," I said with a nervous glance at the sky. Lightning streaked across the clouds again, and here I was under a damn tree. "Look, he might not show it, but Rafe is just happy to be there. He enjoys our company."

"Hmm. Not that you can really tell."

I huffed out a laugh. "No, he is a bit of a grumpy bastard, isn't he?"

"That's one word for it."

"Well, whatever word you choose, I know he'll be happy with whatever you do. Make him his favourite coffee walnut cake. Or buy him some socks. You know crazy socks are his thing."

A smile bloomed wide across my lips. Knowing that Rafe Scott, purveyor of scowls and frowns, wore brightly coloured cartoon socks underneath his dark designer suits and Amiri jeans made me stupidly happy for some reason. No one ever would have guessed, and yet I knew that small, secret part of him. Few people had that privilege.

The speaker crackled while my mum hummed in thought. "I suppose you're right."

"I am." Another rumble of thunder had me bracing despite the slowing patter of rain on the leaves above. Every year I wished for snow and every year I got… this. *Stupid, annoying British weather.* "Anyway, Mum, I gotta go. I'll be there on Sunday. You better have those roasties stacked up ready for me."

Mum chuckled. "I will, darling. See you then. Love you. Bye!"

"Love you, too."

One damp tube journey and two drinks later, I sat in the corner booth of a basement bar in Covent Garden, squinting through the darkness at my boyfriend across the table. The music was a cheese grater against my already irritated nerves, but the seats were comfy, and they served good cocktails and fries here. Again, it was all about compromise. Something had to give, and tonight it was my eardrums.

"Say again?" I near shouted, leaning forward to hear better while I scraped back my damp, frizzy hair into a ponytail as best as I could without a mirror.

"I think we should break up," Michael repeated.

Yep. I'd heard him right the first time.

"You're dumping me?" I asked needlessly and laughed into my cosmo before taking another swig. This day was shaping up to be one for the books. The shitty book where everything shitty happened.

Michael winced at the thud of my glass hitting the tabletop. I should've known. He'd signalled his intentions pretty well when he sat on the opposite side of the booth – it might as well have been a mile away – and hadn't removed his coat, still damp and speckled with rain. He'd looked everywhere but at me as I'd ordered our drinks, even though I hadn't seen him in three weeks and this dress made my boobs look fabulous. Okay, so I had a whole drowned rat vibe going on currently but still. I couldn't even remember if he'd touched me but that didn't bode well either.

Shit.

"I'm sorry, Tee," he said, though his tone betrayed him.

"It's Talia," I replied flatly. Only my siblings called me Tee, and that was because our younger brother, Jacob, couldn't pronounce my name when we were kids.

Michael huffed. "There's no need to get snippy. We can be adults about this. I just think we've run our course, you know? Things have been a bit… stale."

I blinked at him, irritated by the way his nose wrinkled in disgust when he touched the tabletop. I wasn't about to admit we'd *run our course* three months ago. Or pretty much a month after we'd started dating. Or that the word *stale* was being generous. I'd blame myself for staying too long in another dead-end relationship tomorrow, and all the days after that.

Tonight was for wallowing and drinks.

"Okay," I said with a shrug, then knocked back the rest of my drink. Tilting my head back, I held the cocktail glass upside down and opened my mouth wide.

"Stop that!" Michael hissed, glancing at the neighbouring tables as I wiggled my tongue out to catch the last drop of alcohol as it rolled down the rim. Eh, whatever. I was jobless now, which meant I was going to savour every last bit of this ridiculously overpriced cocktail because it was probably my last for a while.

I'd have to go back to my budget student diet of baked beans on toast and cheap bottles of vodka that tasted like nail polish remover. Or worse – no booze at all. No more designer shoes or handbags. No more ordering food in. That stupidly expensive anti-ageing eye cream would have to go too. Not that it did anything. Money was about to be tighter than the current pinch of Michael's mouth.

Fuck. Jobless.

And now boyfriend-less.

On the same damn day.

Life was great sometimes until it wasn't.

My laugh sounded empty and flat, a mirror of my insides. I glared across the table. "If I'm embarrassing you, leave. No one's stopping you. The door's right there."

"So that's it?" Micheal's eyes widened. "Six months over, just like that? No discussion about it?"

I couldn't believe the gall of the man. "I told you I lost my job and your response was to dump me. Forgive me if I'm not in a chatty mood. And if you expected me to beg, you don't know me very well. Also, don't forget, we can be adults about this."

"Wow." He sat back, the leather seat squeaking slightly. "You really are a heartless bitch."

I wasn't. I knew I wasn't, but my heart caught the jab anyway. There were a million ways I could've lashed out, but I refused to give him the satisfaction by sinking to his level. Instead, I swallowed the sting, smiled, clutched my chest and said, "Aw, thank you!"

Michael shook his head. "Whatever," he mumbled and slid out of the booth to leave. "Thanks for nothing."

I discreetly gave his back the middle finger before I grabbed the bar food menu. *Fuck it.* A portion of fries was cheaper than a cosmo. If I couldn't get drunk on alcohol, I'd get drunk on carbs.

CHAPTER 2

RAFE

Fucking bullshit.

I slammed my phone face down and took a swig of beer, though it did nothing to dilute the annoyance burning the back of my throat. The first chance I'd had in weeks to hang out with my best friend, have some beers and decompress a bit, and now this shit? Unbelievable.

"What the hell was that?" Leo shouted at the TV, throwing both arms wide. "It's clearly offside. Wanker."

Almost half-time and Chelsea were down 2–0 against Liverpool. A looming defeat never left Leo in the best mood. Me either, most of the time. Our football obsession was half the reason we'd become such good friends. Except tonight I was too distracted to care. My foot bounced a jittery beat on my knee, too irritated to stop.

I had a problem.

A major fucking problem.

My phone buzzed again. Case in point. I already knew what the text would say. Just another variation of what I'd been told multiple times in the last month, but I'd dragged my heels. Ignored it at every turn. Tuned it out at every meeting. Now it was about to bite me in the ass.

Henry: You have one week, Rafe. Please bring that girlfriend of yours this time. Loosen your tie. Also would it kill you to smile?

It might, Henry. It fucking might.

"Tell them how you really feel," I said, shooting off a reply.

Rafe: I will deal with it. Go home to your wife already.

"If you stopped looking at your phone for one minute you'd see I was right," Leo replied, not once taking his eyes off the screen as he reached for the last of the spring rolls.

I glanced at the coffee table strewn with leftovers and the six-pack of beer we usually would've demolished by now and, well, he had a point.

"Says the guy surgically attached to his phone. Who is it this time, huh? Anna? Lola? Or was it Grace?"

Leo stiffened. He rarely spoke about his love life and, to be fair, I rarely asked. But I knew enough. Grace was the one who got away.

"I don't want to talk about it," he dismissed me. "Anyway, you know I never text during the game. It's sacred time."

Another point.

"Sorry, mate. It's my CFO busting my balls over this Christmas party next week. He won't shut up about me bringing my girlfriend."

That snagged Leo's attention. Not surprising. The last time I'd had anything resembling a committed relationship I'd been the younger side of thirty and now forty was around the corner. I'd once thought being CEO would give me more time to have a life, maybe settle down. The naivety…

"You have a girlfriend?" Leo asked, his expression and tone riddled with doubt.

"Do I look like I've had time for a girlfriend?"

"I'm not answering that."

"Fuck you!" I said with a laugh.

"Just calling it like I see it." He threw me a shit-eating grin. "Dial it back though. Why do you need a girlfriend to go to a work party?"

"I don't usually. But you know the hotel in Hertfordshire we're trying to buy? The owner is reluctant to sell. Henry thinks inviting him will give an idea of our family-orientated brand, whatever that means. I don't know. People want to relax and loosen up at a Christmas party. How can I sell a brand when Ted from Accounting gets so drunk, he gets his ass out?"

"He's still doing that?"

"Every fucking year. It's basically a Christmas tradition." We laughed at the absurdity, but it was true. A few pints and the man was an ass-flashing menace. I probably should've fired him years ago, but I couldn't deny I got a laugh out of it. Not much achieved that. "I don't know. The whole thing is a bad idea."

"Sounds like corporate bullshit if you ask me."

"That's what I said. And then he bought my dad into it."

"Oh man."

"Exactly." I scowled at the memory and downed the rest of my drink. I resented the implication that my father did a better job, even though our profits at Regency-Scott hadn't fallen once since I'd taken over the family business five years ago. If anything, they were increasing now we'd branched out into smaller boutique properties. Sometimes Henry liked to push me.

I hated to admit it worked.

"Where does the girlfriend come into it though?" Leo asked.

I winced and scrubbed a hand down my face. The question I'd been dreading, but it was my own fault. I'd started it.

"So here's the thing." Shifting forward on the sofa, I

focused on picking at the label on my beer bottle. "I might've mentioned I had a girlfriend... called Talia."

Bracing myself, I spared my best friend a glance.

Expressionless, Leo stared at me for one long, excruciating moment before throwing his head back with a laugh. "Oh man. Of all the names, you pick that one?"

"It just came out." I couldn't tell him the real reason. "You think she'll be mad?"

"I don't know. Depends on the day. You know what she's like."

I did. As much as I'd fought my attraction over the years, something about Talia spoke to something in me. A kinship, a mutual awareness, I wasn't sure. But a connection was there, and it had lingered long enough to make a mark. Long enough that I thought about her. A lot. Sometimes I'd go weeks, even months, without seeing her and still felt like I knew her to her bones, like we could pick up exactly where we left off. Any time Leo mentioned his sister, I absorbed the information like a sponge, needing any sign that she was okay, happy.

It didn't help that I knew what she tasted like, how incredible her body felt beneath my hands. Which was why I was in this mess in the first place.

"Do you think she might help me out?"

"Ask her," Leo said with a shrug, and I was grateful he didn't seem bothered about it. "What's the worst that can happen?"

The last time I'd asked for Talia's help we'd drank too much and shared an unshakeable kiss forever seared into my memory.

"You have no idea," I mumbled.

Ten minutes to full-time – fifteen depending on the ref – my phone rang. I groaned, clenching my eyes closed. As much as we had our disagreements, Henry knew only to call me if it was something serious.

But when I caught sight of the name on the screen my pulse quickened: Sunshine. I glanced at Leo; his own phone silent beside him on the sofa.

Why is she calling me and not her brother?

"Doesn't Henry realise it's Friday night and some people have social lives?" he said, popping open another beer. The lid clinked and rolled across the floor somewhere.

"Is that what we're calling this?"

He rolled his eyes. "Tell him to fuck off."

"I've tried. It only makes him more determined and more annoying. I'll be right back. Record the end for me, would you?"

"You're kidding." Leo gestured wildly at the TV, throwing me a look of disbelief as I left the room.

"Talia," I answered as I entered the kitchen, far enough for privacy but still close enough that paranoia kept my voice low. "Is everything okay?"

"Heeeyyyyy," she sang. "Who's this?"

"It's Rafe," I said slowly.

"Rafe! Hi. How are you? Why are you calling me?"

The way her voice brightened around my name had me pressing a fist against my smile. "You called me, remember?"

"I did?" She sounded so shocked I almost laughed.

"Yep."

"Oh my god. I'm so sorry. I'm…" She inhaled so deeply she hiccupped. *Fucking adorable*. "Carbs weren't cutting it so I had to have the hard stuff, y'know."

"I can tell." The oven clock read 9:30. Somehow, this phone call would've made more sense at 2 a.m. I'd definitely hovered over her name in my contacts on more than one occasion in those early hours, especially after a night of drinking. Loneliness hit harder when it felt like the world was asleep. "Are you okay?"

"Me? I'm fine," she said, but her pitchy tone sounded more like *I'm dying inside.*

"You know, when people say they're fine, it usually means the opposite, right?"

"Okay, Detective. You got me. You solved the case. Whoopdee doo!"

I chuckled. "Well, almost. How about you tell me what's wrong and then I'll close it."

Talia fell silent and I straightened from my slump against the kitchen counter. "Are you in danger?" I demanded, unsettled by the way my heart had relocated to my throat.

"Why do you always think the worst?" she grumbled.

"I think it's warranted in this instance. Is it wrong to worry about you?"

"No, no... It's nice that you worry. Or that you care enough to worry," she added quietly.

My stomach lurched. How she thought I didn't care enough was beyond me. But then I remembered the way she'd looked at me when I told her our kiss had been a mistake. Something had twisted painfully in my chest every time I'd thought about those shiny eyes, for weeks afterwards. Maybe even months. Hell, even now.

"Of course I care," I settled on, trying to figure out the best way to phrase it. I'd lived to regret hasty words between us before. "I know we've not spoken in a while but I'm always here for you. We could go a year without speaking and I'd still be there. Whatever you need."

Another beat of silence bled down the line, then...

"I got fired today," she admitted, so soft I almost didn't catch it over the loud cheer seeping in from the other room.

Leo whooped and clapped while his sister's heart ached like a fresh bruise.

"I'm so sorry. What can I do?"

"Nothing. I just needed to tell someone, you know? And I thought, who can I tell who won't make me feel like a failure? And I thought of you."

She thought of *me*. Fucking hell, I felt ten feet tall.

"You're not a failure."

"I guess," she said with a half-hearted sigh. "But my parents are going to be so disappointed in me."

Impossible. David and Joanna Johnson were some of the best people I knew. Leo and Talia (and Oliver and Jacob) had won the parent lottery. There was no way they'd ever be disappointed.

"How bad is that?" Talia carried on. "Thirty-five years old and I'm worried about what my parents think. Embarrassing."

"Wanting to please your parents doesn't magically switch off in adulthood." Something I knew all too well. Unfortunately.

"Well it should because this feeling sucks and I don't know how to stop it."

I ached to hold her. Take her in my arms, crush her to my chest and whisper that everything would be okay. I rarely felt helpless, but I had no idea how to give her the comfort she needed. I scowled at nothing and everything, all at once.

"Are you sure there's nothing I can do?" I asked.

"There's nothing *to* do. But I feel better for telling someone. Now I'm going to drink the night away to forget for a while. And I'm cooking microwave fries. Well, obviously not cooking. More like zapping. But whoever invented these deserves an award, like how amazing to have fries in ninety seconds." A faint ding in the background. "They're ready!"

A smile broke out across my face. If anyone could make me smile, it was her.

"You know what would go great with those fries?" I suggested.

"Oooh, what? Tell me."

"Water. Drink some now. I'll wait while you do it."

"You're so bossy."

I rolled my eyes but felt pretty satisfied by the sound of running water. "Now fill the glass again and put it by your bed. Maybe grab some paracetamol too. Tomorrow's Talia will thank me."

"Can I thank you now, for answering?" she asked after gulping down some water. "I know you're a busy bee. That's why I called because I'm a busy worker bee too. We're the same like that, always buzz buzzing around. I knew you would understand, y'know? One workaholic to another."

I frowned. She was right – I rarely had a spare moment to even think – but it was unsettling. The me of twenty years ago had never planned to be so work-focused. It had just happened. As the only child of William Scott, it wasn't like I had any choice in the matter.

"Well, maybe you can take this as a sign to take some time off," I said. "Regroup or whatever."

"Ha! I wish. But I'm not that brave." She went quiet again. "I'm never brave."

I didn't like the sadness working its way into her voice. "Talia – "

"Anyway, I'm gonna go now," she added brightly, like she'd shrugged it off and pulled herself together somehow. "Bottles to drink, tears to cry. Thanks for listening. I'll be seeing you, Rafe."

"You can count on it."

"Hmm."

"You can count on it," I repeated adamantly, seconds before she hung up.

I stared at my phone until the screen darkened, unsettled in more ways than one.

Still dazed and disconcerted, I walked back into the living room. Leo was relaxed on the sofa, cradling a beer, feet propped on the coffee table while he watched the post-match talk.

"Did you get everything sorted?" he asked.

"Almost." Not even close. "Score?"

"2–1. Sterling came in at the final minute."

"I thought we'd won with the noise you'd made." I flopped onto the opposite end of the sofa and stretched my arms behind my head. We watched in silence for a while before I asked, "Do you think I'm a workaholic?"

Leo's laughter stopped as soon as he realised I wasn't joining in. "Oh, you're serious?"

"Why is that funny?"

The pointed lift of his brow said *Dude, really?* "You spent the whole game on your phone and missed the end to answer a call you could've sent to voicemail, and you don't think you're a workaholic? Didn't picture you for stupid."

"Okay, easy now. Point taken but there's no need to be a dickhead about it."

"I'm just saying. Switch it off every once in a while and maybe your bed won't be stone cold."

I scowled because, yet again, he had a fucking point.

Maybe it was time to change that.

CHAPTER 3

TALIA

Christmas decorations at my parents' house came out on December 1st, so the front hedge was decked with multicoloured lights when I arrived on Sunday afternoon. A wreath of blue pine, dried glazed orange slices and cinnamon sticks hung slightly crooked on the front door. Through the front room window, the Christmas tree and fireplace garland were sprinkled with white lights. Despite the ache in my chest, the weighty gloom lightened at the comfort the entire picture held.

Dorothy was right. *There's no place like home.*

Sometimes.

The ruling part of me dreaded stepping through the door because the pretence would be over. I'd have to admit out loud the reality that had gnawed at me since Friday afternoon.

I'm thirty-five years old with no job and no idea what to do next.

Unfortunately, my parents didn't help. My youngest brother, Jacob, had once been out of work for three weeks, and my dad had worried so much about what it meant for his pension credits he'd started having chest pains. I dreaded to think what he'd say now.

"Did you forget your key again?"

Rafe's voice saved me from that worrying thought, and I spun in time to catch his graceful climb from his Audi convertible, along with my eldest brother, Leo. The pair were similar in height, both over six feet, but where Leo was a closely shaven dark blond, Rafe's was thick, chestnut brown, artfully dishevelled and sweeping above his grey eyes.

My heart stuttered at the sight of him.

All broad shoulders and stubbled jawline, his cheekbones looked chiselled from stone. He had a tiny bump from a broken nose he was self-conscious about – he'd mentioned scheduling plastic surgery more than once – but I thought it gave him character. I often imagined tracing it with my fingertips while he told me the story of how it happened. I'd never admit it because we weren't like that. We didn't do things like that.

One drunken kiss five years ago notwithstanding.

Five years…

Time had made things easier in some ways. The frustration that he'd never see me as anything more than his best friend's sister gradually faded to a sad sort of resignation, but every now and then I was punched with the full weight of everything unsaid.

I like you. A lot.
Sometimes I think you like me too.
Sometimes.

This time of year was the loudest of them all.

But then I remembered all the things he did say after he'd kissed me like he'd been drowning and I was the only air.

I made a mistake.
We can't do this again.
I'm sorry.

I pressed a hand to my heart. The ache of those words like a bruise that never healed.

"Tee!" Leo shouted when he noticed me paused at the gate, loud enough to shake me from staring longingly at his best friend with his stupid broad chest and arm muscles perfectly filling out a black cashmere sweater. With his dark jeans and leather jacket, Rafe looked especially scrumptious today. I stifled a groan.

"How the hell did you get here first?"

"I'm as shocked as you are."

My brother grabbed my face and kissed my forehead with a loud and exaggerated "Mwah!"

"Ugh, stop!" I said with a laugh, shoving him away as he walked down the garden path to let himself into the house. *Nice to see you too, bro.*

In the silence Rafe stepped by my side, his presence as warm and powerful as if I'd looked right at him. But that was the thing about Rafe Scott, he could command a room without so much as a word.

"Hi, my little worker bee," he said with a knowing grin.

Worker bee?

The way his smile deepened only confused me more. "Uh, hi?"

"What are you doing out in the cold?" he asked, the accusing demand alleviated by the soft kiss he pressed to my cheek.

"Oh." I blinked a few times against the heat of Rafe all up in my personal space and had to hold back another lusty moan. I wanted to fix my nose right up to his neck, inhale deeply, and sail away on his delicious scent. Instead, I nuzzled into the depths of my woollen scarf. "Just admiring the decorations. Mum's gone for coloured lights this year. I think I'm in shock."

"Huh. What happened to her no-mixing-coloured-lights-with-white-lights rule?"

"Your guess is as good as mine. Never thought I'd see the day."

Rafe huffed a laugh through his nose, soft and soundless. His gaze travelled all over my face, like he was memorising every detail, though that didn't seem possible. "It's good to see you," he admitted a beat later, and the warmth of it flooded fizzy joy into my veins.

"Ditto," I said with a smile.

Our eyes met and held.

The last time I'd seen Rafe was after I'd announced my new relationship with Michael at one of my family's Sunday lunches, five months ago now. I often wondered if that meant anything, whether he was jealous or couldn't bear to see me with another man, but that was wishful thinking. Rafe was a busy man and probably felt the same as my brothers: annoyed I was settling yet again for someone who wasn't right for me.

Story of my life.

Rafe looked away first, clearing his throat. "So," he started as we made our way down the path. "How are you today?"

Now that was a question.

"I'm... okay." I forced a smile. "You know me. Plodding along."

He watched me closely. "You don't remember, do you?"

"Remember what?"

"Calling me on Friday."

I halted on the path. *Oh my god.* Friday night wasn't just a blur, it was no longer part of my memory. I'd left the bar safely and halfway to sober, but everything after that? Gone. The only indication I'd spent the night drowning my sorrows were the two empty bottles of wine I'd dumped in the recycling bin the next morning, the dull ache blooming across the back of my head. I'd also slept with one arm still in my dress, presumably having wrestled enough with the zip trawling my spine. *Disaster.*

I'd barely recovered, even now.

"I embarrassed myself, didn't I?" I scrunched my eyes closed for a second. "I suppose the upside is I don't remember, so that's something."

Rafe chuckled. "You called yourself a worker bee. Why did you think I called you that?"

"No idea." My cheeks heated thinking about what else I might have said. *Oh god.* "Can you have second-hand embarrassment about yourself? Is that a thing?"

"I don't know. You were pretty adorable, if you ask me."

Adorable? Just what I wanted to be called by the man I longed to climb like a tree. "That's not helping," I said with a groan, covering my face with one hand.

"Seriously though, I was sorry to hear you lost your job. We didn't get a chance to discuss it properly, but if they didn't give you a reason, I think you have a real case for unfair dismissal."

"Oh." I scraped my fingertips roughly across my forehead. "I fully unloaded on you, huh?"

"I didn't mind."

"Either way, it won't happen again. But thanks."

"Talia," he said, tugging on my wrist as I started to walk away, and I looked down, both startled by the alien sensation and delighted by it. "It's going to be okay, you know."

I shook my head, then dropped my gaze to his boots. His voice was too soft, too kind, and I was a shiver away from crying. "You don't know that."

"But I know you."

He gave me one last squeeze before heading into the house, and I stared at my fingers, wondering how long the imprint of his touch would last this time.

As the rich scent of roast beef drifted above our steaming plates, my mum wandered into the dining room sporting her favourite festive Minnie Mouse apron and set the china gravy boat on the table. Her short, greying hair was fastened into a stubby ponytail, her hairstyle of choice when cooking over a hot stove, and she took a moment to fan her flushed face with a tea towel before throwing it over one shoulder.

"Now that I have all of my children here," she announced, holding up her empty glass in Leo's direction. "I'd like to talk about Christmas."

A joint groan of varying octaves swept across the table.

"Don't you and Dad want to have a quiet Christmas to yourselves this year?" Leo said first, dutifully filling Mum's glass with white wine.

I narrowed my eyes at him. I wasn't sure what he was up to but now was my chance and I jumped at those. "That would be lovely, right? A small, quiet dinner just the two of you. No annoying men hogging the remote and cheating at Monopoly. Sounds like bliss, if you ask me."

"No one asked you though," Oliver said with a shit-eating grin, jerking out of the way when I threw a solid punch at his arm. Three years older than me but anyone would think it was the other way around.

"Plus, it's not cheating if you're that good you win every year," Jacob added smugly. "Not that you would know."

"Oh be quiet. I let you win."

"Sure you do."

My younger brother was too far on the other side of the table, so I settled for giving him the middle finger, a gesture he delighted in, throwing one right back.

Rafe stared at his plate, failing to hide his amusement.

"I love your father very much but I can't think of anything

worse," my mother said honestly while Dad gave a nod of agreement. "I have 360-plus days just the two of us. Christmas is about being together as a family. I thought I'd have grandchildren to play with by now but – "

Another round of groans while my stomach plummeted to my feet.

"I mean, really," she carried on, "three grown children in their thirties and one who is forty and not one of you has given me a grandchild yet? What did I do to deserve this? David, pass the salt."

"I'm too young to settle down," Jacob said around a mouthful of carrots. "Sorry."

"You're thirty," Dad replied, pushing the salt shaker down the table.

"Exactly. Ask me again in ten years."

"Hopefully you'll have matured by then," I added.

Jacob grinned, tipped his glass in the air, and winked.

"Spoken like a man who has all the time in the world." Mum huffed, wielding her fork with all the emphasis of a dagger. "You can go around producing sperm for years and years, but I don't want to be an old granny. At this rate I'll be ancient."

I gulped down a too-big mouthful of wine, enough that I almost choked.

"Joanna, dear. Can we not talk about sperm at the dinner table?" Dad asked, giving me a steadying pat on the back and shaking his head the way he always did when things got out of control.

This happened a lot.

I sat stiff as a board, anxiety clawing at my throat. My mother voicing one of my deepest fears was the icing on the crappy cake that was the last few days. I had yet to admit it out loud, but the truth was I wanted a baby and was no closer to having one now than I was six years ago, when I'd first started to think about the idea seriously. Children had always been a far-off eventuality I hadn't given much thought until I was staring the big 3-0 in the face and all the decisions that came with it. Figuring out I wanted kids was one thing. Realising it might never happen was another. I didn't need the reminder. Not today.

My gaze darted to Rafe sitting opposite. Something fluttered in my chest when I found him staring, but I grimaced, mouthing *sorry*. This couldn't have been the most comfortable conversation to witness, even if he was used to it.

Rafe shook his head, his smile soft enough to settle the tension that had climbed into my shoulders two days ago. Despite his persistent moodiness, he always seemed to have a calming effect on me. On tougher days all I wanted to do was run straight to Rafe and sink into his solid arms. Everything felt like it was going to be okay when I was near him. That's all I needed. To be adjacent to Rafe.

Maybe that's why I'd called him drunk off my face. The less I thought about that, the better.

"Are you bringing Matthew to Christmas this year?" Mum asked.

"Michael." I followed my weary sigh with another swig of wine. "His name is Michael, and no. I'm not." I found myself staring at Rafe as I added, "We broke up."

The flare in his eyes was my imagination, I was sure of it. A trick of the light.

"Oh, darling," Mum said. "I'm sorry."

"I'm not," Leo scoffed. "That guy was a dick."

"You met him one time. And yes, okay, he was a dick, but even so. You spoke to him for like five minutes."

"I knew it in two," he replied, stuffing a whole roast potato in his mouth and staring at me while he chewed.

My nose wrinkled in disgust. I didn't know why but whenever we sat for dinner we all morphed into our teenage selves, the table some twisted kind of time machine. I couldn't call them out on it because I'd acted the same on more than one occasion.

This was why I needed a break.

I couldn't be dealing with this now. I wasn't sure I had the strength to plaster on a smile and play happy families full of Christmas joy when all I wanted to do was crawl under my duvet and cry. It was all part of my process. I needed to break before I could mend.

Rubbing my hands down the sides of my face, I heaved a long, drawn-out sigh. My pulse raced at what I was about to say. Or rather, the bomb I was about to detonate. At least that's what it felt like.

"While we're on awkward subjects, I lost my job on Friday," I admitted to a round of shock and commiseration from all sides, and my skin burned hot with adrenaline. *I did it! I admitted it.* "For restructuring reasons apparently, which is Nadia talk for you're too old. Oh, and then Michael dumped me. Not that I care because we weren't right for each other. But now that's out there, I won't be here for Christmas either. Anyway, what's new with you?"

There was a round of clinking as everyone's cutlery clattered to their plates. Almost everyone. I could feel the strength of Rafe's gaze on the side of my face as I nibbled on a chunk of cauliflower.

"What?" Mum said quietly, but there was something lethal in the sound, so much so that I let my gaze circle the rest of the table first, dreading my mother's reaction.

There was nothing worse than being a disappointment.

Everyone looked at me in a mixture of confusion and disbelief, which wasn't surprising. None of us ever missed Christmas. Not once.

Until now.

I glanced at Rafe. The almost permanent furrow of his

brow seemed deeper somehow, sharper, and I would have given anything to know what he was thinking.

"Talia Louise Johnson, I know you didn't just tell me you're skipping Christmas," Mum scolded.

"I love how that's all you focus on," I mumbled while my mother looked seconds away from a coronary.

"Talia!"

"Mum, Dad, I love you, I love all of you, even you," I added, glaring at Oliver. "But I'm not in the mood to celebrate this year. I just want to be alone. I need some space to think. There's a lot going on in my head right now."

"You're being very selfish."

"Mum," Leo warned, and I appreciated that one word more than he'd ever know.

"Yeah, maybe I am. So what? Why is needing alone time selfish? I know you'll get mad if I sit here moping all Christmas. Surely it's better if I'm not here to do that."

"Nothing's more important than being with family," Mum said haughtily.

"I'm more concerned about the job," Dad joined in, fingers clenched around his napkin. "What are you doing about that? Do you have anything else lined up? What do the job listings say?"

I pinched the bridge of my nose and closed my eyes. "I don't know yet, Dad. Okay? I don't know. It happened two days ago. I'm still catching my breath."

"But surely – "

"Please," I whispered desperately, tears stinging beneath my eyelids because I still hadn't processed the loss of my job, the terrifying prospect of my future, and what the hell I was going to do now. Michael didn't come into it aside from a vague kind of annoyance but that was mostly at myself, as predicted.

I've wasted so much time...

Surprisingly, my dad's hand settled on top of my own, loosening the fierce grip on my wine glass. He gave me a gentle pat before staring down the table at his wife. They communicated silently for a few seconds, which seemed to settle my mum somewhat.

"What will you do?" she asked, mystified. "Sit in your flat alone?"

I sighed for what felt like the millionth time, incapable of anything else. "Yes."

It wasn't like I had any other options.

❄

A couple of hours later, I filled the kitchen sink with warm water and soapy bubbles. After dropping that bomb at dinner, the washing-up was the least I could do. I felt like punishing myself for some reason, even though I hadn't done anything wrong.

What was so wrong with needing space?

Part of me was also desperate to avoid the inevitable job discussion with my dad. I'd already caught him looking at job adverts on his mobile, and the sight had me fleeing the room.

"Here, let me," Rafe said softly, nudging my hands away from where I was trying to tie the apron behind my back.

"Thanks," I said, my breath quickening at the feel of him behind me, slowly looping the strings into a neat bow at the base of my spine. Hyper aware that he was likely staring at my ass. Everything he did was so methodical, but it set on me edge in ways I didn't know were possible, didn't truly understand. My swallow was more than a little ragged when he settled his hands on my hips, gave me a soft pat and said, "All done," right against my ear in that low, gruff tone that always made me shiver.

I clenched my eyes closed.

He was close, too close, and why did he have to touch me like that? Like the curve of my hips were a perfect fit for his hands? Like he wanted to memorise the shape of my body through touch alone? He'd done that once and look what happened.

Instead, I said, "I'll wash, you dry?"

"Sure." Rafe grabbed a tea towel from the counter, grinning at the material dotted with cartoon reindeers and Christmas stockings. My mum went all out. Even the toilet paper was patterned with candy canes and gold stars.

We worked together in comfortable silence, the kind that came with familiar, monotonous tasks with friends. The TV was a distant murmur in the living room along with my brothers arguing about Chelsea's latest match. By the third plate, Rafe said, "Were you serious about being alone this Christmas?"

If only. A dreamy sigh drifted out before I'd thought about it. "If I could get on a plane and fly away tomorrow, I would. A girl can dream, right?"

"And it's important to you? To get away?"

"I'd like to. I mean, obviously I won't be going anywhere but... I don't know. I need a change. I think I'm still in shock. I never expected it. I've never been fired in my life."

"Your boss is an idiot."

I'd heard Nadia called a lot of things over the years, but *idiot* was a definite first. "You've never even met her," I said with a grin. "But I agree."

"Don't need to. I've heard enough horror stories from you over the years. She's a tyrant."

Understatement.

"What's worse is that she spoke about promoting me," I admitted, which I hadn't told anyone. I only shared good news once there was some. Thank god. "I could probably get over the firing if it wasn't for that. I keep racking my brain trying to figure out what changed. Was it anything I did or said? It's a mind fuck."

"So she promised promotion and sacked you? Fucking asshole."

Rafe scowled down at the measuring jug, wiping it dry with more roughness than necessary. My chest warmed at his annoyance on my behalf.

"And Michael..." he added as I passed him another plate. "Must've been tough."

"Eh." I would've flapped a dismissive hand if it hadn't been wrist-deep in sink water. I'd barely thought about the man. "That should've ended months ago. It hurt the way he did it, but that's about it."

Rafe nodded distractedly. "Right."

"You think I'm terrible, don't you?" I asked, cringing. "That I'm not bothered about my boyfriend."

"Ex-boyfriend." Rafe turned to me fully, fist braced on the counter. "And the way I feel about you is the complete opposite of terrible, Talia."

WHAT?

My heart jumped right into my throat.

What does that mean?

My eyes felt as wide as dinner plates. Rafe's gaze settled briefly on my lips and flitted away, as it always did when things grew too intense, too close to that line we'd crossed once before. I wanted to grab him by his collar and rattle him, shake out all the answers to my questions somehow. But I didn't. I *wouldn't*.

"So," he began, clearing his throat. "I'm aware that now isn't the best time, but I have a favour to ask and I'm realising there's a way we can both get what we want."

"Colour me intrigued. I'm listening."

"How do you feel about being my girlfriend?"

The plate I'd been washing plopped into the sink,

sloshing water over the sides and soaking the front of my apron. "Excuse me?"

Rafe looked like he was struggling not to smile, a magnificent sight. I wished he did it more often.

"Pretend girlfriend, I mean. I need a date for my Christmas party."

"And you want *me* to be your date?" I double-checked, trying to ignore the well of disappointment. *Of course he didn't mean real girlfriend, Talia. Idiot.* "What do I get out of it?"

"A date with me, of course."

"You arrogant bastard," I said with a smile.

"I'm kidding." He held up both hands in mock surrender. "How does staying in one of my hotels sound? Or maybe my cottage in Scotland? You're welcome to use it."

"Oh." That was unexpected. "Really?"

"It's all yours. Just say the word."

"You're serious?"

"When am I not?"

Considering I'd barely seen his face without a frown, he had a point. "I don't know what to say."

"Say yes."

Could I?

A remote Scottish escape sounded like perfection. A change of scenery and the space and quiet I needed to clear my head and sort my life out. Or at least plan how to do such a thing. Right now, I had no idea. Running away to Scotland also meant there was no chance my mum would turn up at my flat and guilt me in to attending family events – a high possibility.

"When is this party?"

"Friday. I figured you could fly up to Glasgow that weekend. It gives my housekeeper time to get things ready for you up there."

"You have a housekeeper? No, wait. Of course you do."

"Not on site. She lives in the village and keeps it clean and stocks the fridge ready for guests."

"Right. Of course." I nodded along. Occasionally, Rafe didn't live in the real world with the rest of us. "Dress code? For the party, I mean."

"Whatever you want."

"Well, I don't want to turn up in my ugly Christmas jumper if everyone else is wearing a ball gown or something."

"Ballgowns aren't really my style."

Despite myself, I laughed. "Shame," I found myself saying. "But you have a deal."

He simultaneously lit up and sagged in relief, which I found strange but didn't question. I couldn't imagine Rafe struggling to get a date. He was the kind of man who turned heads in his direction. "Great. I'll text you the details."

"Are you sure about the cottage?" I asked again. "Your parents don't need it?"

"You know my parents always spend Christmas in the Caribbean."

"Will you spend it with them?" I wasn't sure why I asked. With the exception of one year, Rafe had spent every Christmas with our family since we'd met. He even had a stocking hanging above my parents' fireplace. Whenever I thought of Christmas, Rafe was as much of a tradition and memory as everything else. Baking cookies, watching *It's a Wonderful Life* and *Home Alone*, wearing terrible Christmas jumpers and Rafe, almost smiling back at me across the table, beating me at board games, and letting me use his shoulder for my after-dinner snooze.

It would be hard not to have that this year, but I also wondered how many more years I could take being so close to the man and not in the ways I dreamed. I wanted him to hold my hand under the table and kiss me awake and never tell me goodbye.

My heart was weary. As the years passed, I waited on edge, certain Rafe would show up with a serious girlfriend and I'd have to watch him settle down and build a life – a family – with someone else. His happiness meant everything to me, but the thought was as brutal as a knife in my side.

"No," Rafe said. "I think I'll do the same as you. Spend Christmas alone."

"You know you're always welcome here, right? My parents love having you. We all do."

"I know. But you're not the only one who needs a break," he said, heaving a weary sigh.

"Is everything okay?"

"Being the boss is exhausting sometimes, that's all."

There was more going on but Rafe only confided when he was good and ready, so I let my other questions slide. "I can only imagine. Are you sure you don't need the cottage for yourself?"

"One hundred per cent. I want you to have what you want."

He reached for my hand and I watched his thumb drift back and forth in a soft, unknowing caress, slowly meeting his eyes. Mere seconds, and there it was again. That attraction. Like a crackle in the air. So palpable, surely this was the moment we'd lean forward and our mouths would meet again, at long last… Until my mum walked into the kitchen carrying more dirty plates, and our connection shattered, too brittle to do anything else. Rafe shifted away, grabbing a wet saucepan from the rack and carrying on as if nothing had happened.

Same old, same old.

"Oh, you don't have to do that, Rafe," Mum said, sliding between us to dump the dishes by the sink. "You're a guest."

"But you cooked. And you've always told me I'm not a guest. That I'm family."

Mum's cheeks tinged pink. She'd blame the wine if asked. "Well, you've got me there. If you want to help, who am I to stop you?"

We made quick work after that, in silence, the way it always was after we'd shared another moment – an almost moment – thwarted for the thousandth time.

"So," Rafe said once he'd tucked the last plate back in the cupboard. "I'll pick you up on Friday?"

I nodded, exhilarated by the thought but also wary, wondering what I'd just exposed my heart to. "It's a date."

CHAPTER 4

❄

RAFE

I'm screwed.

From my car I watched Talia glide down the front steps of her building in those spiky heels she loved as much as I loved what they did to her ass. Tonight the ribbon ties matched her dress, winding her ankle the way I'd like to wind my fingers around her wrists. Maybe the strands of her hair as I tugged her head back to kiss her full, lush mouth.

I remembered that mouth…

"Fuck," I whispered roughly, clutching the steering wheel in some semblance of calming the fuck down.

Too late for that.

She always looked good but tonight was something else. Her hair was half up, half down, loose waves brushing past some kind of wrap too thin to keep her shoulders warm. But that dress… As red as cherries, modest as it reached past her knees but utterly obscene in the way the silk slid like syrup down her curves. And Talia had those in abundance. I swore under my breath again. *Get it together, Rafe. Just get it together.* Eventually, I remembered my manners and jumped out of the car, charged with a lethal cocktail of adrenaline and nerves. *Excitement.*

I'd spent countless hours with this woman, knew the exact measure of her smile and the genuine sound of her laugh, that blue was her favourite colour and she never went a day without listening to music, all these minor everyday details that made up a person. But tonight was the first time it would be just the two of us since the night we'd kissed and I'd ruined everything. The shift felt monumental somehow.

I'd waited for this day even though I never thought I'd have another chance.

"Hi," she said brightly, all glossy red lips and glittering eyes.

Definitely screwed.

"What's wrong?" she asked, glancing down at herself, tracing the low neckline of her dress before smoothing a palm down her hip a couple of times.

"Nothing. You look... You're perfect," I managed, voice croaky with disuse. I couldn't admit she'd taken my fucking breath away.

"Oh, thank god. You were scowling at me again. I thought I was overdressed or something."

"Impossible."

"Though I suppose I'd rather be overdressed than under-dressed. Nothing worse than turning up to a black-tie event wearing jeans." She paused, startled. "It *is* black tie, right?"

"It is," I confirmed with a smile, gesturing at my own black suit. "And I don't believe you've ever done that."

"Oh, I did. Back when I first started working for Nadia. You should've seen her face." Talia visibly cringed at the memory. "Now that I think about it, I'm surprised I lasted as long as I did."

"Don't sell yourself short."

She shrugged, her mouth turned down like *oh well.*

I studied her for a long moment. She'd seemed so strained the other day. Even if she hadn't drunk-dialled me, I would have known something was wrong as soon as I saw her face. "You sound more like yourself. You feeling okay?"

She forced out a laugh. "Oh, not at all. But this is supposed to be a party so tonight I'm Party Talia. Mopey Talia will take over later when she's no longer in public."

"Well, Party Rafe is grateful but doesn't think you should hide your feelings. So if it's a shoulder you need to cry on, mine's free."

"There's a Party Rafe? I'm going to need some proof he exists."

"Don't get too excited. He only comes out when he needs to."

Talia ducked her head to laugh. "You're sweet. But I'm fine. Or I will be." She frowned. "I think…"

"I *know*." I squeezed her arm, wishing it was her hand. "Are you ready?"

"Yes, but first…" She wrestled with a tiny strapless bag she'd tucked under one arm and pulled out a silk tie, the red a shade darker than her dress. "A Christmas present. Well, part of it. I thought as I won't be seeing you this year, you could wear it tonight. My mum and dad are always wearing matchy things. Maybe we'll look more like a real couple?"

My pulse liked the sound of that, maybe too much with the way it throbbed at the base of my neck.

"It's silly, isn't it?" she added in the face of my silence, shaking her head and refolding the tie. "You don't have to. It was just an idea. I don't – "

"Stop." I touched her hand, drawing her eyes back to mine. "I want to."

I stared at her long enough that she stepped closer and lifted the tie over my head, smoothing it under the collar of my black shirt. I wore ties usually, so Party Rafe had been going for a more relaxed, open-collar look tonight – per Henry's request – but right then I would've worn anything she'd given me.

Fucking Party Rafe. What the hell.

Talia's forehead wrinkled in concentration as she looped the tie over and under, and I couldn't take my eyes off her lips. The space between us felt like nothing at all, and after years of enforced distance on my part, it was almost too much. I drew in a sharp breath, louder than intended, and Talia's gaze flew to mine, hands faltering for a second. So much was volleyed back and forth in that endless stretch of a moment.

Do you still want me?
Do you feel it too?
What are we waiting for?

Talia's throat rolled and I knew she felt it too. That awareness between us never went away, no matter how many boyfriends she had, no matter how many girlfriends I'd tried, however much I wished the attraction would die back in those early days of mine and Leo's friendship. He'd been the closest, most honest, friend I'd ever had and fuck if I was going to ruin that. But all these years later, it was still there and wasn't going away. If anything its presence was stronger, more feral somehow, and I wasn't sure how much longer I could keep it locked inside.

Why was I even keeping it inside? I'd forgotten the reason.

Leo?

But he would understand. I was sure of it.

My time-consuming job?

That wasn't going anywhere. But Talia would be if I didn't get my act together. She'd already slipped so far away.

"Rafe…" she whispered, and I would've stolen that breathy taste of my name if she hadn't shivered in my arms.

I cleared my throat, the sound as ragged as I felt. "It's freezing. Let's go."

❋

"So who is it that we have to schmooze tonight?" Talia asked, tucking her arm into the crook of my own. She gazed around slowly, her face lighting up whenever she caught sight of something she liked.

There wasn't a corner of the ballroom that wasn't decked out for Christmas. Pine garlands with gaudy red baubles and white lights draped from the ceiling. Red and green wrapped boxes with gold and silver bows were stacked as centrepieces on every table currently set for our three-course meal. A huge spruce tree towered in the corner by the dance floor that wouldn't be empty for long. I scowled at the sight.

Myself excluded.

I didn't dance and never would.

"Schmooze?" I threw a nod at Henry over by the bar, my expression falling into something less polite when his wife Ingrid lit up at the sight of Talia by my side. Like a shark at the first scent of blood. *Shit*. "Is that what we're calling it?"

"Sure. What else?"

"I'm thinking more a brief conversation where I highlight all of my charms."

"Oh really? What would those be?"

I grinned down at her tucked by my side. "It's a long list. You might want to jot this down."

"Oh, shoot. Forgot my pen." She fisted the air with an *aw-shucks* kind of gesture, a smirk playing at her mouth. "Does the arrogance come as standard with the suit or is it just you?"

"It's in the lining."

"Stop it," she said with a laugh. "What's this guy's name?"

"Alan Fraiser. He's heading this way right now."

Talia straightened at the sight of the short, balding man walking towards us, like a switch had been flipped. *Showtime.* She set her face with a bright, easy smile and nestled closer, enough that her breast pressed against my arm. I clenched my jaw, gritting out a smile that probably looked as awkward as it felt.

This is torture.

"Anything else I should know?" she whispered.

"He's family-orientated. Old fashioned. Outdated. You name it – Alan," I greeted loudly as he approached, shaking his outstretched hand. "Welcome to Regency-Scott. I hope you're enjoying yourself so far. Have you had a tour yet?"

Alan straightened his bowtie – red to match the festive braces peeking out of his suit – and glanced around the room, nudging the bridge of his glasses as they slipped down his nose. "Yes, yes. Very impressive. You've outdone yourself."

"I have a great team. One that could be yours if you came onboard. Just say the word."

He hummed, a dismissive, doubtful kind of sound. This wasn't going to be an easy sell.

"By the way, I'd like you to meet Talia." I didn't blush but my body temperature definitely ticked up a couple of points when I added, "my girlfriend."

"Oh, you're not married?" Alan looked between us, his brow furrowed. "Henry mentioned you've been together a long time."

Talia cast me a confused glance. "Uh, not yet."

"Well, you don't want to wait too long. You're not exactly getting any younger, are you, boy?"

Boy. God, this guy was a dick. "I'm not even forty. Don't write me off yet."

Alan laughed awkwardly. "Yes, of course. You're right.

Some of us got married at twenty-one, that's all. I can't imagine waiting as long as you."

My jaw tightened and I knew I wasn't the only one tired of this conversation. Talia had gone rigid by my side, her smile no longer meeting her eyes. I linked our hands, weaving our fingers together.

"I think life would be pretty boring if we all ran at the same pace, don't you think?"

"Yes, well," Alan stuttered, finally realising he'd put his foot in his mouth. "Perhaps I'll get Henry to give me that tour now."

"Perhaps you should," I said.

Talia waited until he was out of hearing distance. "Well, that went well," she said. "Dickhead."

I huffed out a laugh.

"Are you sure you want to do business with him?"

I glanced back at Alan talking to Henry at the bar and grimaced. Right then, I wasn't sure at all.

❇

Dinner was the usual gourmet cuisine followed by a speech I was forced to choke out every year. One of the worst things about being CEO was the public speaking. I'd rather eat my own foot. I held up my glass in thanks to the round of applause and made my way back to Talia seated at our table, still savouring her chocolate dessert even though dinner ended a while ago. I felt like the luckiest guy alive to be the recipient of that smile.

The music switched to something slower, smoother, meant for not much more than swaying. I couldn't take my eyes off Talia's face as she watched the couples partner off, moving in their own worlds.

"Would you like to dance?" I found myself asking.

What the fuck?

She looked like she'd had the same thought. "I... I didn't know you could dance."

"I'm not sure I can," I admitted with a wince. "Wing it with me?"

"The best kind of dancing if you ask me," she said with a laugh, sliding her hand into my own. "Let's go."

I led her to the dance floor, rolling my eyes and shouting, "Yeah, yeah, whatever," at the whoops and cheers from my employees at the shocking sight. *Shitheads.* I stifled a grin at Talia's giggly gasp of delight as I spun her out before twirling her back into my arms. She wasn't expecting the manoeuvre and collided with my body with a breathy, "Oh!" that went straight to my cock. My mind jumped to all the other ways I could draw that sound from her, maybe something that would have her neck thrown back in ecstasy, clutching at my hair. I'd run my tongue down that arch too because Talia's neck was prime for my mouth, my hands, a necklace of diamonds and definitely pearls...

Fuck. I needed to control myself. Concentrate on something – anything else. A few of my employees watched at the edges of the dance floor and even over by the tables, and it must've been weird for them to see me with a woman, and definitely dancing with one. I'd only ever come to these events alone. Now, I'd turned something that shouldn't be a big deal into a mystery to solve, a spectacle to witness.

But it felt like a big deal with her in my arms. The generous swell of her breasts and the soft slope of her lower belly pressed up close, all made a million times worse by the scent of her perfume. She'd intoxicate even the sternest of men.

Even me.

There was a hesitance in the way Talia reached for my shoulders, as if she knew the touch was dangerous to my sanity. She drew in a breath when my hands settled right where I'd longed to touch all evening, that mesmerising curve of her hip where it melted into her waist.

"So," she said when we started to move, swaying back and forth. I could sway as much as the next guy. "What are the chances Alan might sell?"

"Slim." I was even more convinced since his continued dismissal over dinner. Every time I'd broached the subject, he'd changed it. "I told Henry this was a waste of time, but he never listens to me."

"Strange, considering you're the CEO."

"You think?" I shook my head, frustrated. "He was so far up my dad's ass, sometimes I think he's got shit in his eyes. I don't think he has any faith in me."

"But it's been, what? Five years since you took over?"

"Almost six."

"Well, speaking as someone who has been replaced at work, Henry needs to realise there are plenty more CFO's in the sea, so to speak."

I chuckled. "At this rate, I'll retire before Henry does. I swear he comes with the building."

Talia breathed out a soft laugh, ducking her chin, and the top of her head brushed my jaw. Some strands of her hair caught on my stubble, and I smoothed them away. Her gaze immediately found mine and the air between us shifted in a blink, crackling with awareness as I gently tucked those strands behind her ear.

"Thanks," she whispered, blinking up at me like she was as frozen as I was.

I couldn't do this much longer. I couldn't.

It was one thing to manage with time and distance but another when she was right there, walking by my side, talking to the people I worked with daily, slotting in like she'd been here the whole time.

"I don't know about you, but I could use a drink," I said as the music changed to something more upbeat.

"I could definitely use a drink," Talia muttered. "Or five."

At the bar I ordered a scotch and a white wine, glancing around the room, trying and failing not to think about Talia in my arms, while she chatted with Ted from Accounting who, thankfully, hadn't flashed his ass. Yet.

I'd barely handed Talia her wine when Ingrid marched over to join us, pushing everyone else aside. She was almost as tall as me – with short platinum blonde hair and a dress the colour of the Merlot sloshing around in her glass – and unbelievably irritating, like the buzz of a fly that wouldn't leave the room.

"Hello," she drawled, her German accent all but disappeared now. "We didn't get a chance to talk at dinner, unfortunately. I'm Ingrid. Henry's wife. You must be the girlfriend?"

My grip tightened around my glass.

"I prefer Talia."

"I've heard so much about you," Ingrid replied.

I stiffened while Talia blinked a few times, her brow lifting in surprise. "All good I hope."

"Oh, Rafe raves about you constantly. Talia this, Talia that. Isn't that right, Rafe darling? We wondered why it's taken all these years to meet you."

"Years?" she repeated, throwing me another startled look.

Shit. "I'm sure it hasn't been that long," I bit out, knocking back the rest of my scotch.

"I was pregnant with my youngest when you first mentioned Talia and he's six now, darling." Ingrid shook her head, rolling her eyes. "We've been waiting with bated breath for so long."

The hardness that flickered across Talia's face was gone in a second. "You must think I'm so rude. I'm so sorry."

"Not at all," Ingrid dismissed with a flutter of fingers weighed down with diamonds. "More intrigued than anything. We started to wonder if he'd made you up."

She cackled like she'd cracked the best joke in existence, but when Talia turned to me it wasn't amusement firing in her eyes.

❋

Henry was in the process of telling Alan about his family's plans for Christmas, but I was too distracted to do anything but nod along.

Usually Talia's smiles were blinding, painted on no matter what, but now one barely reached her eyes. Her cheeks only flushed when she drank too much or was angry about something, and she'd barely touched her wine. More than once her gaze flittered to the exit, and I felt a surge of panic that she was about to run. Stupid because she'd never do that. Talia stuck to her commitments no matter what. There was no real risk she'd leave and yet... My hand curled into a fist. All this talk about Christmas and New Year plans pissed me off. I didn't fucking care. I needed to know what was wrong.

I'd formulated three different reasons to excuse us both when Talia said, "If you'll excuse me, I need some fresh air."

Everyone carried on as if it was no big deal, but they didn't know Talia. I threw out a quick apology and followed her determined march outside, unsettled by the shake of her head, the swaying clench of her fists. She was *mad* mad.

Outside, the terrace was all dark corners and shadows and overlooked The London Eye; the pods lit a bright, neon blue that hurt my eyes while they adjusted to the lack of light.

"Talia," I said, conscious of the cold but also grateful for it because it meant we were out here alone. Thank fuck.

"I need some air," she said quietly, curling her arms against a shiver, the cold turning her words white. "Go back inside. I won't be long."

Goosebumps scattered across her skin, barely visible in the sliver of moonlight.

"It's too cold out here." I started to shuck off my suit jacket, but Talia shook her head and another step away.

"Don't," she blurted.

My stomach sank. "What did I do?"

"It's what you didn't do, Rafe."

Well, that pissed me off. "Meaning?"

She huffed, frustrated. It was pointless trying not to reply. I was a dog with a bone when I needed answers. Someone had to stop and it wouldn't be me.

Talia folded her arms and sent me a fierce, challenging look. "How long have you been telling everyone I'm your girlfriend?"

"Oh. That."

"Yes, *that*," she said flatly. "How long?"

I blew out a breath. How the hell could I answer this and come out unscathed? Impossible. "I don't know? A few years maybe."

"A few years," she repeated. "Wow. No wonder Ingrid was surprised I was here. The elusive girlfriend finally shows her face. They must think I'm an asshole."

"No one would ever think that about you."

"Michael did. He said I was heartless. And if someone I'd been sleeping with could think that about me, imagine all the strangers in there."

"Well, Michael's a fucking idiot," I snapped, furious she'd even mentioned his name. I didn't need the blatant reminder rubbed in my goddamn face either. "And he's irrelevant. Don't mention him again."

Talia turned sharply. "Don't tell me what to do."

"Okay. *Please* don't mention him again."

"Oh, much better," she said, rolling her eyes. "The *please* really softens the blow."

"I thought so."

"Rafe…" Despite herself, a weak smile broke out across her face, impossible for her to stay mad. She shook her head – at me or herself, I wasn't sure – and curled her hands around the railing as she stared out at the River Thames. The wind sent her hair fluttering behind her, and I closed my eyes when I caught all that floral scent that was just… Talia.

I'd once followed that scent around my local supermarket convinced it was her even though she lived nowhere near me. My disappointment when I couldn't find her had been eye opening. I'd thought about the reasons for months afterwards.

"I don't understand why you used me as your fake girlfriend. After everything that…" She shook her head. "You could've made one up."

"I could have. You're right. But why does it matter?"

Her gaze turned razor sharp. "Excuse me?"

"It's not like it's affected your life in any way." The truth. I'd been throwing her name around for years and no harm had come from it. "Until tonight you had no idea. Why are you so angry?"

Her mouth opened and closed, then, "I don't like people thinking I'm rude! Everyone thinks I've ignored invitations to your work events, like I don't give a shit or something."

"No they don't. And who cares if they do?"

She pinched the bridge of her nose, like I wasn't getting it. "I just would've appreciated all the facts. You know how I feel about being blindsided."

Deflated, I couldn't argue with that. "Okay, that's fair. I should've told you. I'm sorry."

"Thank you."

"But there's more to this. I know you."

Talia's gaze drifted away.

"You've never been this angry at me before. Tell me why," I insisted, stepping closer.

"I don't know."

"Yes, you do."

Silence.

When she looked up at me, all I could think about was how close she was, how beautiful she looked, how much I wanted her to be mine. It must've shown on my face somehow, in the way I inhaled or maybe it was the step closer, right up into her personal space. I'd never know what gave me away. All my focus remained on the widening of her eyes, the flit of her gaze to my mouth, the way her tongue licked at her lips like an invitation, a silent request I couldn't deny.

Our mouths collided.

A roughened groan left my throat as Talia curled her tongue against mine. *Finally.* I grabbed her face, my fingers a hard bite against her cheek, harder than I'd ever imagined, but I couldn't help that fierceness if I tried. Desperation burned in my chest as I moved her head exactly how I wanted it, a better angle for our mismatched heights, and licked into the shuddery gasp that bled from Talia's mouth.

If she wanted to be handled, I'd fucking handle her.

My other hand inched down her spine, learning the path of all that bared skin, still warm despite the cold, and clutched greedily at the delicious swell of her ass, more than a handful. More than two handfuls. I was an ass man and Talia's filled out her skirts and jeans in a way that made me want to pray on my knees as if I did that sort of thing. Maybe bite down on my fist instead of the bite I'd like to print into one fleshy cheek, and not the ones on her face.

Fuck.

Instead, I squeezed again and again, couldn't get enough,

and Talia wrenched me closer, something mindless in the way she moved. Part of me had always been concerned she wouldn't be able to deal with me or the roughness I couldn't hide, too much sunshine for my shadows, but here she was, matching my every move, wreaking havoc inside my suit jacket. She clutched at my sides, my belt, then around to my ass, like she couldn't make up her mind where to start, what to brand first.

Everywhere. Touch me everywhere. It doesn't matter. It never did.

I'd take anything.

Everything.

Just don't fucking stop.

Somehow, I managed to tear my mouth away, a thread away from losing my damn mind. I smoothed one hand down her body, rubbing the hem of her dress between finger and thumb.

"Talia," I breathed out, shaking my head slowly. "What am I going to do with you?"

Breathless, Talia took a few seconds to answer, and I held still waiting for her response, for the moment we changed everything. If we hadn't done that already. She'd either give me the green light or tell me to get fucked. I was on the edge – a knife's edge, a cliff, I wasn't sure. The edge of something.

Something real.

Her eyes glittered in the low light. "You tell me."

Biting back my roar of triumph, I gathered the silky material high enough to slide my hand underneath, electrified by the touch of all that smooth skin in a place I'd only ever seen from afar, always *look, but don't touch*. An overload of wanting, years of it, flooded my senses as I brushed my fingers back and forth, and Talia made a throaty sound that screamed *more, I need more*.

The world darkened.

Nothing else existed but this moment, this woman, right here and now.

I grazed my knuckles higher up her thigh, slowly, drawing out the tease because I liked that, and the way it made her shiver, until I met the edge of her underwear. I followed the elastic path all the way back until it reached between the cheeks of her ass all bare for the taking.

"You wore this to drive me out of my goddamn mind tonight, didn't you?"

"No," she breathed out, eyes glued to my mouth. "I – "

I grabbed the thong and tugged it to one side. How I resisted the urge to tear it off her, I didn't know. My restraint felt as taut as an elastic band and any minute now... *Snap*.

"Admit it," I demanded, loving the shiver that rolled through her limbs.

"I dress for me." Talia rocked her hips, trying to force my fingers lower. "Anything else is a bonus."

"Liar," I whispered, bringing our lips together in another frantic kiss. For a second, a lifetime, we were nothing but a breathy mess of grunts and groans.

Everything buzzed and hummed. I was more adrenaline than man.

I *couldn't* wait.

Crowding her against the wall, I settled one arm above her head and dipped my fingers into the wet of her sex, gratified by her harsh inhale. I swiped around her clit a few times, teasing, before cupping her fully. I didn't intend for it to feel like a claiming, but it felt like one anyway as she sank into my touch and all I could think was... *Mine*. I didn't move for a long moment and Talia rocked against me, pulling away to release another breathy moan that had my cock swelling against her thigh. Any thoughts I had about drawing this out disappeared the moment she whispered my name, rough and desperate against my cheek.

I slid two fingers inside her and she clutched wildly at my arms.

The sounds of the city were nothing but white noise in comparison to the rough scrape of brick against Talia's back, the wet sound as I fucked her with my hand, our heavy breaths. I'd dreamed of her like this, and she was everything I'd imagined and more.

"Look at you clenching down on me already," I murmured in awe, groaning at the sensation. How great that would feel around my cock. One more roll of my thumb over her clit, and she came, barely making a sound except for a stilted garble in the back of her throat. "*Fuck* yes. Beautiful."

Once wasn't enough.

Everything was still pulsing and wet when I pressed against the spot that made her gasp and rubbed quickly back and forth with the heel of my hand.

"Rafe, it's too much," she pleaded, squirming as her body danced that line between pleasure and pain, right where I wanted her. Out of her damn mind, like I was. "I can't, I can't!"

"You can," I gritted out. "Fucking come for me."

Her head rolled back, her hair a static mess, and my lips found her neck as I licked that promised path down her fluttering pulse point, desperate for more and –

"Whoops!" A voice echoed out across the terrace, and for that one never-ending second I couldn't move. The thought of someone else seeing Talia writhing against me, an image meant for me alone, had every muscle tense with alarm.

NO.

"Sorry, didn't mean to interrupt. Carry on!" A fresh burst of giggles faded as the door swung closed and everything stilled except the pulse of Talia's pussy.

"Don't stop," she begged, still rocking back and forth, and

of course I couldn't stop when she looked at me like that, all desperate eyes and kiss-bitten lips.

It was the whispered *please* that did it. Pure, unfiltered need that fired something in me. Redoubling my efforts, I thrust into her with three fingers now, circled her clit with my thumb over and over, until she screamed silently into my chest. She scrunched my jacket in a white-knuckled grip as she shuddered and soaked my hand for the second time in as many minutes.

Hottest thing I'd ever seen. Bar nothing.

I was hard as steel, sweating patches through my shirt. I groaned as I pulled my fingers out and stared down at Talia slumped against the wall, breaths still heavy, lipstick wrecked. Her dress was yanked up to her waist, and her skin-coloured thong a tangled scrap where I'd shoved it to one side in my desperate haste. Her thighs quivered as she struggled to hold herself up, and the whole thing was so obscene I wanted to go again and next time it would be more than my fucking hand.

I couldn't.

I shouldn't.

Not right now anyway.

Now that the intensity had faded, the outside world filtered in. We were out in the open. I didn't recognise the woman's voice from moments before – likely another hotel guest – but any one of my employees could've walked out and seen me fucking Talia against the wall, because that's where it was heading. Normally I wouldn't have given a shit, but this was still a work function and there was a time and this definitely wasn't the place. Talia deserved soft sheets and I deserved a bed to wreck, like I'd always pictured.

We'd both be a wreck by the time I was finished.

"Rafe?" she said throatily, voice hoarse, brow furrowed. "What's wrong?"

"Nothing. But I did just fuck you up against the wall in plain sight."

"I know, I was there." She played with the length of my tie, plucking the end. Her grin the kind of flirty that I wanted to fuck. "If it wasn't obvious, I liked it."

"Fuck." That was doing nothing to help the situation in my pants. I took a step back. Maybe some distance would rewire my brain from my cock.

"Right. Okay." Talia hastily righted her thong and tugged her dress back down her thighs, smoothing the fabric a couple of times. "That's how this is gonna go."

What?

"No, I – "

"It's fine. It was another mistake. Message received."

"What the fuck? Message not received."

"It's my own fault. I should've listened to you the first time."

"Talia!"

She flew inside and I ran my hands down the side of my face, startled by the scent of her still on me. I should've been sucking on her taste right then, should've watched her suck the taste of herself too as I forced my fingers into her mouth. Not this. Never this.

I kicked the leg of a nearby table. "FUCK!"

I gave myself a few minutes to get my act together, but it was hard when my suit was rumpled by her, and I could still feel the print of her mouth against mine. Eventually I had to button my suit jacket and hope for the best.

When I reached the entrance to the party, Talia appeared from the restrooms, fussing with her dress and hair even though she looked perfect.

Perfectly fucked.

"We need to talk," I said.

Talia heaved a sigh. "I know but not now. Let's go inside

and play happy couple for the rest of the night. You have a deal to finalise."

"I don't give a shit about the party anymore. Or that fucking deal. It's a lost cause."

"Don't be ridiculous. I know it's important to you. And I'm not going to be the one who drags you away in front of all your employees."

"Talia."

Fucking look at me.

"Can you do this or not, Rafe? I know I can."

My jaw clenched. She wasn't going to let this go. "Fine. We'll talk later." I reached for her hip but she pulled away.

"No, don't touch me please."

I dropped my hand because of course I did but –

"How am I going to sell this if you won't let me touch you?" I was pushing it, but I couldn't help myself. Being told I couldn't touch this woman after I'd touched her so intimately was something my brain and body couldn't reconcile. I wasn't sure how the hell I managed to do it all those years before.

But maybe I hadn't managed at all.

Maybe I'd been lying to myself.

Talia looked at me, absolutely nothing in the smooth slope of her expression. "You've managed to sell it pretty well without my even being here, so I think we'll do just fine."

She marched back inside and headed for our table, smiling at Alan as she struck up a conversation with his wife. I shoved my hands into my pockets, rooted to the floor while I dialled back the compulsion to follow her. What the hell was I going to do now?

❄

Alan Fraiser was more than merry a couple of hours later; his joy the excuse I needed to take Talia home. We drove in a silence so thick it felt like a suffocating second skin, and when I pulled up outside her building, she had the seatbelt released before I'd switched off the ignition.

"Thanks for the lift," she said, seizing her clutch from the footwell.

"Sure. Thanks for coming with me tonight."

She nodded. "Alan seemed to enjoy himself. I think he'll be selling. Mission accomplished."

Doubtful. "We'll see."

Another moment of silence so awkward I wanted to rip my face off. This wasn't us. We didn't do awkward silences. Unsaid words, maybe, but never that.

"When's your flight?" I asked, inwardly rolling my eyes at the nonsense question I didn't give a shit about. But I needed more time. I had so much to say but couldn't say any of it knowing she was about to run away. She had that restless air and one hand already reached for the door.

"Tomorrow morning."

"You'll let me know when you arrive at the cottage safely?"

"Of course. And thank you again. I appreciate you letting me stay there."

"You still want to go?"

"Now more than ever."

My mouth tightened. "Okay then. Call me if you need help finding anything. Any time, night or day. I'm here."

"Thanks," she replied, but I knew she wouldn't. Not now.

I leaned across the console to kiss her cheek, but Talia swiftly opened the door to escape, leaving me hanging. Outside, she bent down to look through the door, her gaze seemingly everywhere but on me.

How could I have gone from the hottest moment where

everything felt so fucking right to... *this?* Talia Johnson not even looking me in the eye. Maybe this is what I'd been trying to avoid all these years. A little part of Talia was better than nothing.

"Have a nice Christmas. Good night."

She slammed the door and rushed up the steps to her building. The shawl slivered from her shoulders and fluttered in the wind. I watched to see if she'd turn back – a single glance would've been enough, would've been *something* – and waited until the inner car light switched off and Talia had long since disappeared.

After, I sent Leo a text telling him we needed to talk and drove home as empty as the seat beside me.

CHAPTER 5

TALIA

The jingly, tinny sound of *"Last Christmas"* greeted me first, followed by a fallen rope of sparkly, purple tinsel as I entered the village shop. I flicked it away, too distracted by the text that had popped up on my screen.

Rafe: Please, Talia. Tell me you're OK.

The same as all the other messages he'd sent, it made my stomach drop and my heart soar – a true chaos of emotions. I'd been trying so hard not to think about him – an impossible task when I was staying in his cottage and sleeping in his bed – and now he was texting me wondering if I was okay.

I wasn't sure how to answer.

The kiss we'd shared five years ago paled in comparison to the taste of him now. In retrospect, last time had been nothing more than a drunken fumble. Kisses stolen between sleepy smiles and laughs, tentative caresses of my waist, and fingers drifting through my hair. Back then it had been electrifying – Rafe Scott, finally touching me. Kissing *me*. I'd thought it was the start of something instead of the end of it. A line drawn in the sand.

But this time...

He'd consumed me. *Devoured.* There was no other word for it. I knew now how it felt to be wrapped solidly in his arms. Knew the feel of his mouth along my neck, the warm caress of his breath across my skin. Nothing would ever shake or erase the memory of his fingers inside me. *Nothing.* The moment, the feeling, was forever ingrained.

I also knew the fierceness with which he moved, the strength of his grip against my face, and the claiming bite of his fingers as he'd squeezed my ass. The control, the mix of power and thinly veiled restraint. Rafe had touched me like he couldn't get enough, like he wanted to worship at the altar of my body.

How was I supposed to forget and move on? How could I look him in the eye across the dinner table and pretend I didn't know the sound of his roughened groan as I came all over his hand? The feel of him hard against me.

My sex clenched just thinking about it.

Impossible.

My world had shifted. This was an after-Rafe existence and there was no going back.

So no. I was not okay. I wasn't sure I ever would be.

And I didn't know how to tell him that. Not without giving my heart away, and he wasn't having that. Not now.

I huffed, frustrated, and shoved my phone in my coat pocket. My reply would have to wait. Right now, I had supplies to buy. When I looked around to get my bearings, my eyes widened. Christmas had vomited everywhere. Tinsel ran along every shelf edge and counter. Strings of sparkly baubles hung from the ceiling, swaying gently in the fresh breeze I'd carried inside. Fairy lights twinkled and faded and flashed in different patterns all over the place.

A plump, middle-aged woman with greying curly hair and kind eyes gave me a cheery nod. "Hello, dear," she said in a thick Scottish accent, zipping her lilac quilted body warmer all the way to her chin. "I'm Mrs Brown. How can I help?"

"Hi." I smiled, grabbing a basket. "Do you have flour and vanilla essence? And chocolate chips?"

"Of course. Middle aisle, bottom shelf."

I slowly made my way along each narrow aisle, throwing in whatever caught my eye. The cottage had a fully stocked pantry and I'd already purchased supplies, but sometimes a girl needed to make cookies. Maybe not the cute Christmas-shaped cookies I'd been making with my mum every Christmas Eve since I was old enough to hold a wooden spoon, but right now any cookie would do. I'd make them the size of my head, too. Maybe have them for dinner because why not?

"Are you the one staying up at Chestnut Cottage?" Mrs Brown asked, adding, "the old Scott place," when I looked confused. I didn't realise it had a name.

"Oh yeah, that's me. My brother's friend owns the place. Or his family do? I'm not sure."

"His parents used to own it. Rafe bought it from them."

My gaze flew up from the row of chocolate bars. "You know Rafe?"

Her pointed look said *puh-lease*. "Of course. You should've seen him stomping around here when it happened. That cottage has been in the Scott family for over one hundred years. He was furious they wanted to sell."

Poor Rafe. God, his parents sucked. "I can imagine."

"It all worked out though."

Did it? I lifted my basket onto the counter and threw in a couple of sharing size chocolate bars. I'd be sharing those with myself later. Mrs Brown shook out a bag and started ringing up my items while I stared unseeing at the wall lined with cigarettes.

There was so much about Rafe I didn't know, and despite everything, I still wanted to find out.

Would that feeling ever pass?

"Now, while you're here, I think you should take a bag of gritting salt for the driveway," Mrs Brown said. "There's a snow storm headed our way."

"There is?" I asked brightly, excited for the first time all week. The prospect of a real white Christmas made me want to jump with joy. "I'm not going anywhere so it's fine."

"Oh no, dear. You need to be prepared. We don't want you stranded out there by yourself. You've seen what that road is like. I'll give you our business card in case you need anything."

"Thank you," I said, tugging out my credit card to pay. "How long does the snow typically last this time of year?"

"Depends. Sometimes months."

Wow. Okay. "You best give me some of that salt then."

❄

Chestnut Cottage was a fifteen-minute drive from the village and nestled against a backdrop of rolling green hills and distant snow-capped mountains. No other property in sight. I'd wanted peace and quiet and I was getting it.

My stomach lurched and tumbled but I dismissed it quickly. The time for regrets was gone.

I grabbed my shopping bags from the rental car and paused to take a deep breath, spluttering a cough at the itch in my throat. Even though it had been a week, I was still so unused to the bite of clean, fresh air.

I definitely wasn't in London anymore.

The cottage loomed behind me, larger than I'd originally pictured. I wasn't sure why. Rafe's family were millionaires so naturally they wouldn't own anything small. Probably didn't know the meaning of the word. Even so, the word *cottage* always gave off a snug, cosy vibe in my imagination and this was anything but. The outside appeared stark against the hills, but when it snowed – fingers crossed – it would completely disappear into its surroundings, if not for the grey roof and royal blue front door. There was a matching garage set back to one side and a couple of shed-type buildings further back. I still needed to explore those later.

Some wooden outdoor furniture, in desperate need of sanding and a lick of paint, sat at the front, and I'd spent every day so far sitting there wrapped in a blanket, basking in the view of the loch further down the valley. The first day I'd cried, the kind of deep, wrenching sobs that made my sides ache and my face puffy for hours afterwards. But still, I persisted. Nature always had a way of reviving my mind like nothing else, and I needed all the help I could get if I wanted a plan formed by the time I returned to London.

All I'd managed so far was writing the word "PLAN" as a heading on the first page of a new notebook. Underlining it twice.

Dumping my shopping in the kitchen, I grabbed that notepad and spent the afternoon reworking my CV – twenty solid years of working since I was fifteen meant it took a while – and the only conclusion I made was that I wanted to stay in PR. But who would hire me now? Getting sacked from anywhere was never a good sign but getting sacked from NT Public Relations was the darkest mark of all.

I threw the pen across the table and glared as it rolled onto the floor.

❄

The sky was inky blue and dotted with thousands of stars when I turned on the radio and plugged in the KitchenAid ready to make cookies. I danced around the room and by the time the counter was lined with little bowls of measured ingredients, my earlier frustration had faded. I wasn't a cook by any means but baking always brightened my spirits.

"Now," I said to the imaginary audience in the kitchen. "The first thing we want to do is combine the butter and sugar until it's pale and fluffy."

I switched on the KitchenAid, increasing the dial slowly. The contents had barely circled the bowl when everything went black.

"Shit!" The plunge into silence after the whirr of the mixer and music only added to the panic slicing through my chest. "Shit, shit, shit!"

If I'd been at home there would have been some light filtering in through the window from a street lamp or the city outside, but out here in the middle of nowhere? Pitch black. If someone appeared in front of my face, I'd have absolutely no idea.

My insides dropped. Now that was horrifying.

My phone was charging upstairs, but there had to be a torch somewhere. I patted around searching for a handle as if I hadn't been using the kitchen all week, pulling out drawers and slowly feeling my way through the shapes of everything inside. Typically, I found the torch in the last place I looked, and my shoulders loosened at the beam of brightness in the otherwise black room. *Thank god.*

Hand on heart, I allowed myself a few seconds of calm before making my way to the garage, thankful I'd already discovered the mains fuse box was outside. Sometimes it paid to be nosy. The door creaked open. I karate chopped the cobwebs away as they fluttered against my skin, overwhelmed by the creepy spidery sensation.

"It's just your imagination, Talia. Don't even think about it," I said, directing the torch beam at the fuse box on the wall. I flipped two switches and peeked out of the garage, sagging with relief at the warm glow through the windows.

Two steps back toward the cottage and—

What is that sound? I held still for a long moment, not hearing anything new, and rolled my eyes. Being alone in the dark always messed with my brain, no matter how old I was, and knowing there wasn't another house for miles added to the unsettling, ghostly awareness.

Another few steps I was almost near the front door when—

A crunch.

I froze.

That definitely sounded like a footstep this time. It was quiet enough for anything to make a sound but all I could hear was the furious thud of my heart.

I opened my mouth to say hello but stopped myself quickly. *Stupid.* What would I have done if someone had said hello back? Shit myself, probably. No, it was better to not know at all. Even so, the need to get back inside nipped at my insides, adrenaline scorching my veins. I rounded the corner and raced to the front door when the last man I expected to see appeared from the other side of the cottage.

"Rafe? What the fuck!" I pressed one palm to the wall and another to my chest. "I think my soul just ascended."

"Where's your coat?" Rafe demanded, the intensity amplified by the fierceness of his glare. "It's minus three degrees out here."

"That's the first thing you have to say? You scared me half to death."

"I assumed you heard my car drive up." He thumbed at the 4x4 parked behind my car. Well, shit. I hadn't thought to look at the driveway. Barely a week and my usual city-living diligence had disappeared.

"I'm sorry I frightened you," he added.

"It's okay," I said, feeling a little foolish. The cold nipped at my skin, sending a shiver rolling down my spine. I folded my hands into my sleeves and tucked them under my arms. "I overreacted. The imagination goes wild out here."

His breathy chuckle drifted into the frigid air. "I get that. Let's go inside."

I followed him in a daze, stunned by how quickly things had changed and curious as to why. Ten minutes ago my plans for the evening had been cookies and trashy TV, and now Rafe was here, taking up all the space in the living room as if occupying my thoughts wasn't enough.

"You don't have the fire lit?" Rafe wondered while I grabbed the tartan blanket from the sofa and wrapped it around my body, drawing it up over my frozen nose and bouncing in a desperate bid to get warm.

"I don't know how. I was worried about setting the place on fire, so I didn't even attempt it."

He seemed amused by that, even though I was deadly serious. "Come on, I'll show you," he said.

Still in his coat, Rafe crouched in front of the fireplace and began the process of layering logs, rolled up newspaper and twigs into the crate, explaining each step. He reached for the matches on the mantel, lit the newspaper and stood back as the flame climbed higher into the chimney.

"I definitely would've burned this place down."

He laughed, holding his hands up close to the heat, turning them this way and that. "Well, it's a good thing I'm here."

The snaps and crackles from the fire sharpened the silence in the room. My eyelids grew heavy as the adrenaline crashed and the chill began to ease from my bones.

"Why *are* you here?" I asked. "Not that you can't be here of course. It's your place. But…"

"You didn't reply to any of my messages."

I hung my head. "I'm sorry. I was going to, but I didn't know what to say. I guess I needed some time. You didn't need to travel all the way here for that."

"Yes, I did. I wanted to see your face when we talked. I just wanted to talk, Talia. Also, I didn't think it was safe for you to be alone. Actually, safe's the wrong word. I didn't *want* you to be alone."

"What?" I screwed up my face in confusion. "I've been up here almost a week. Why now?"

"You said you wanted time and space to think. I figured a week was enough."

Something about that, respecting my boundaries, my wishes, warmed me inside. "You planned to come up here the whole time?"

"Pretty much," Rafe said, and didn't look the least bit sorry about it.

"But why?"

"I told you. I'm here to spend Christmas with you. No one should be alone on Christmas. You would've regretted it."

"No, I wouldn't." I wasn't about to tell him about the stomach-sinking doubts I'd had that morning.

A knowing look settled on his face. "Yes, you would. Maybe not yet. But come Christmas Eve, you'd have felt it."

"Felt what?"

"The loneliness," he said quietly. "It hits you when you least expect at this time of year. It happens to the best of us. Even those that don't mind being alone most of the time." His gaze drifted to the floor. "Christmas is different."

"Oh."

Inexplicably, my eyes stung. How many Christmases had Rafe spent alone before our family came along?

"You already felt it, didn't you?"

"No," I said weakly. "I've been fine."

"Of course you have. You're the kind of person who'd survive no matter what. But I know you. You need people around you. You're sunshine, and people gravitate to you, they always have."

I watched him intently now, a thrill rolling through my limbs. "You think I'm sunshine?"

"That's my nickname for you."

"You have a nickname for me?" I wasn't sure why that made me so happy, but I felt the pinch of it in my cheeks. "Since when?"

"The moment I first laid eyes on you, walking towards me with the biggest goddamn smile I'd ever seen. You might've noticed I don't do much of that."

"Once or twice." I shrugged, playing it off, all the while my heart felt like it was beating right out of my chest. "Maybe."

His mouth twitched. "That day you wore a pale yellow T-shirt and with your long blonde hair you looked like the sun."

My smile faded at the gravity of his words. The first time I met Rafe he'd looked at my offered hand like he wasn't sure how hands worked. I thought he'd hated me. But I couldn't for the life of me remember what he was wearing.

The importance of this moment shifted something inside me. This was the most he'd opened up to me in years. If ever.

"I would've liked to hear that," I admitted softly.

"I wasn't sure if it was patronising or not."

"I wouldn't have taken it that way at all."

"Well, then." He nodded, a shy smile playing with his lips. "That's good to know."

The width of the room narrowed, stifling all the air as we stared into each other's eyes, wondering who would look away first.

For my heart, I had to.

There wasn't much to say after that. Rafe grabbed his bag from the car while I checked the pantry to see what I could make for dinner. Cookies wouldn't be enough now. I'd settled on soup with toasted cheese sandwiches when a gush of ice cold twirled at my feet and Rafe rolled a small suitcase into the living room, setting it by the stairs.

"Hey, listen," he said. "I know I sprung this on you. If you don't want me here, I'll leave. I don't want you to be uncomfortable."

I shook my head. As much as I'd wanted peace and quiet, Rafe was right. The prospect of Christmas alone was unsettling and now that it inched closer, I couldn't bear the thought. "This is your home. And some company would be nice."

"That's a relief because I'm pretty sure we're going to be stuck here for a while."

I frowned momentarily before rushing to the window in understanding, scooping back the curtain and peering outside. Snow was falling but barely dusted the ground. Disappointed, I let the curtain slide back. "That's a sorry excuse for snow. It'll have melted by morning."

"You wanna bet?"

"Sure. What will I win if you lose?"

Rafe stepped closer, so close I had to arch my neck right back to look at him, our height difference considerable now I was barefoot.

"I never lose," he said gruffly, and somehow I knew he wasn't talking about snow.

CHAPTER 6

❄

TALIA

THE NEXT MORNING I padded down the stairs rubbing one eye, yawning so wide my jaw clicked. My limbs were heavy and sluggish, every step like walking through molasses. I'd been restless knowing Rafe was sleeping in the room next door, replaying everything we'd said and done yesterday, and all the days before that.

I could still feel the ghost of his fingers trailing up my thigh…

"Stop it, Talia," I scolded under my breath.

But… *Sunshine.* He'd called me sunshine.

Something flashed in my peripheral vision and my mouth dropped the moment I turned to find out what. A Christmas tree, so perfect it could've been hand-drawn, sat in front of the bay window, twinkling with hundreds of warm white lights.

"What?" There was awe in my whisper as I wandered closer. I rubbed a spiky branch, then held it to my nose, the scent unmistakable and not at all artificial.

A real Christmas tree.

"Well, that was worth it," Rafe said from the kitchen archway, his head tilted to one side, his smile softer than my heart could take. Steam swirled from his coffee cup and drifted into the air as he lifted it to take a sip.

"What was?" I asked, still dazed and drawn to the tree. I hadn't realised how much I'd wanted – needed – one until that moment. Christmas wasn't Christmas without a tree. I'd been fooling myself to think otherwise.

How did he know?

"Your smile," he murmured. "Worth it."

My heart fluttered like it had taken flight. "How?"

"Mrs Brown can get anything if you ask. I collected it on the way here and hid it in the shed."

So that's what he'd been doing when he arrived and scared me half to death. He'd orchestrated a surprise for *me*. "Rafe, I'm – I don't know what to say."

"Don't say anything. I wanted you to have it. You can't have Christmas without a tree, right?"

"No, I suppose not." I smiled at my feet, weirdly shy all of sudden, overwhelmed by everything and unable to put it into words. "Thank you. This means a lot to me."

I drifted closer, a little hesitant at first, and placed a soft kiss to his cheek, squeezing his forearm, solid beneath the sleeve of his cream Aran sweater. *If he only knew what that sweater does to me.* He smelled clean, freshly showered, and was so handsome it hurt. When I pulled away, Rafe's eyes were closed and only the shift in the air had them snapping open.

"You're welcome," he said gruffly. "I'd do anything for you."

Something flipped in my chest, and I clutched at my stomach as if it could settle the light, floaty sensation lingering inside.

Our gazes held and I blinked up at him, unsure what to

say. How could I respond to such a declaration? And why was he telling me this now?

Rafe broke the connection first, clearing his throat and looking around the room. "Unfortunately, I don't have any decorations. My parents weren't known for keeping that kind of stuff here."

I frowned, remembering the box I'd seen when I opened every cupboard the day I arrived. I wasn't particularly nosy by nature but… it was Rafe. I couldn't help myself.

"What?" he said, sensing my hesitance.

"Um, don't hate me, but I saw a box of decorations in one of the wardrobes upstairs. I'm sorry, I wasn't snooping. Well, I was, but not for secrets or anything. Curiosity?" I winced at the ramble and hid my face behind one hand. "I'm so sorry, I'm terrible."

Rafe laughed. "It's fine. I don't have anything to hide. I'm surprised there's anything here though. I would've thought they chucked everything years ago."

"You might be right. I didn't look inside the box. I'm not that nosy."

"A little bit nosy then?"

"Sometimes. Stop looking at me like that, I'm human. Sue me!"

His wicked grin morphed into a laugh that lit up my insides.

"You haven't looked out the window yet, have you?" he asked, and I startled at the rapid change in conversation.

"No," I said slowly, then raced to the window above the sink. "Oh my god."

"Told you I never lose."

I rolled my eyes, too distracted to form a reply, too delighted by the blanket of white covering everything. Usually this view was lush green fields but now there was no real distinction between that and the sky.

I had snow. I had a Christmas tree. And now I had Rafe, if only for a little while.

"Have you eaten yet?" I asked brightly. Nothing was going to damper my mood today. "How does scrambled eggs on toast sound?"

"It depends. Is this you offering?"

"For the man who bought me a tree? I'll throw in lunch and dinner too."

"So generous," he said with a grin. "How can I refuse?"

"Well, don't celebrate yet," I warned. "My cooking skills are a little rusty."

I grabbed everything I needed from the fridge and dumped it all on the counter while I searched for the pans. My standard method for cooking had always been whatever was quickest and easiest, given I was always squashed for time. So I hadn't cooked anything using the stove yet, more than happy to slip into my usual pattern of something on toast or whatever I could throw in the microwave. But it was different now there was more than one person to cook for.

It felt... nice.

"Bottom drawer under the hob," Rafe said, taking a seat at the kitchen table. "Are you thinking about changing careers?"

"Huh?" I looked over my shoulder to find him peering at my notepad and all the scribbles I'd made about my future. "Oh. I don't know. Maybe."

"But you like PR."

"What makes you say that?"

"You light up when you talk about your work. If you've found a career you enjoy, don't let that demon put doubts in your head."

"Demon," I repeated with a smile. "That's an appropriate name, I think."

"I'm serious. Don't let her shake your confidence."

"Too late." I cracked and whisked six eggs into a bowl,

adding milk and seasoning. "You know, the first few days here I kept imagining Nadia calling me out of desperation to come back. What a joke."

"That's understandable," Rafe said, probably trying to make me feel better. "What did you imagine saying to her?"

"I didn't reach that part. It was always the validation I felt at hearing her beg for my return, that I was irreplaceable."

"You are."

"Ha! She was right in some ways," I carried on, scooping butter into the saucepan and flicking on the heat. "There's always someone better or younger, ready to climb the ranks and take my place. I needed to remember that. Maybe she did me a favour."

"Bullshit. Experience is just as invaluable."

"It didn't help me keep my job though. Now I'm faced with the possibility of being blacklisted. Who's going to hire me now?"

"Then become your own boss."

I paused in reaching for a wooden spoon from the utensil holder. "What?"

"You're worried about getting rehired… Become your own boss."

His tone was a mix between confident and blasé, as if it was no big deal, as if people randomly decided to start their own business every day. But the idea felt monumental and something about it snagged on something in my brain. I trusted my gut instinct about most things and an immediate no was just that. Immediate. End of discussion. But this… this had the potential to ruminate.

"You like the sound of that, don't you?" Rafe said knowingly, his tone tinged with amusement.

I'd gone quiet, too quiet, staring unseeing at the wall.

Was I actually considering this?

"I mean, sure," I admitted and, oh my god, I was. Five

minutes ago the thought hadn't even crossed my mind and now my pulse thundered in my ears at the potential, the possibilities. "I don't know if I have the means to start my own PR business. I wouldn't know where *to* start. There's a lot to consider. Why did you put this idea into my head?"

He chuckled. "I can set you up with my business manager to give you some ideas. If you want."

"I couldn't ask you to do that."

"You didn't ask. I'm offering. Think up some questions, pick her brain. No strings."

"Can I think about it?"

"It would be weird if you didn't."

I knew for the rest of the day I wouldn't be able to think of much else.

❄

After breakfast Rafe made some calls from his temporary desk at the kitchen table while I went in search of the box of decorations.

"I found them," I called out ten minutes later, carrying a battered cardboard box labelled "XMAS DECS" down the stairs. I set it down on the sofa, blowing across the layer of dust on top before thinking better of it.

"Bless you," Rafe shouted from the kitchen at the sound of my eye-watering sneeze.

"Thanks," I managed before sneezing again. The urge tickled the back of my nose twice more, and I held my breath and my hands in front of my face just in case. Once it felt safe, I peeled the yellowing sellotape somehow still keeping the box sealed and rifled through the contents. Red beaded garlands tarnished with age. Matte green baubles. Old Christmas cards cut and hole-punched, then threaded with gold string for makeshift hanging ornaments. I smiled. My mum had once done the same.

"Wow, that takes me back." Rafe walked in as I pulled an angel tree topper from the box. The halo was crumpled and the dress was more beige than the white it probably used to be, but it was still usable. "Haven't seen that since I was a kid."

"Oh, so it's ancient then."

"Less of the old, please."

"I'm four years younger than you. I'm kidding."

He glanced down at the box and went quiet. "Where did you find this?" he asked, picking up a wooden Nutcracker doll missing its nose and half of its moustache. He ran his fingertip down the faded red and gold and stared at it for a long moment, lost in the memory.

"In the top of the walk-in wardrobe in the back bedroom. There's a lot of stuff up there. You should take a look."

He nodded slowly, though not out of any sort of agreement. "I've been meaning to go through everything but I never get the chance to come here. My schedule hates me."

"But you managed to visit now?" I asked, intrigued.

"It's Christmas. And sometimes needs must."

He sent me a long blistering look that heated my skin and forced me to turn away. I refocused on the decorations again, anything to distract myself from all the chemistry making my blood burn like molten lava.

I was going to melt, right here on the floor, if he kept looking at me like that. I wasn't strong enough.

"Aw," I said lightly, holding up a heart-shaped ornament with "Rafe's 1st Christmas" in red lettering, twirling on the string. "This is so cute."

"I didn't know they had anything like that," Rafe said, confused.

"Maybe you celebrated your first Christmas here."

"Maybe."

"You don't know?"

"They've never mentioned it. We don't talk about things like that. I know we spent a couple of Christmases here when I was a kid. That was taken here." He pointed at the tall pine bookcase in the corner and the framed picture of himself and his parents in the snow. He couldn't have been more than five, if I had to guess. It was the only picture in the entire cottage, though I didn't like to think about that because it made me sad to consider the reasons why.

"I didn't realise we spent my first Christmas here though," he said. "I'm surprised."

"Why?" I grinned at the image it made. "Just think, little baby Rafe hung out here. You probably crawled across this very floor."

Rafe scanned the living room, as if seeing it with fresh eyes, and gave a slow, measured nod. "Maybe."

"Right," I said, clapping my hands together, hoping the noise helped disperse the melancholy cloaking the room. "Let's decorate."

"You really want to use all this crap?"

I held the Nutcracker doll to my chest, covering its little ears. "Don't say that. This is what Christmas is all about, as my mum would say."

"Decorations that should've gone in the rubbish years ago?"

"One person's trash is another person's treasure."

He laughed and set about unloading more of the box while I spread a bit of festive cheer around the room. I set the Nutcracker in the middle of the fireplace mantel, tucked around a thin, artificial garland covered in pine cones, and dotted the tree with all of the baubles, even though none of them matched.

"Anything else?" I asked. When Rafe didn't respond, I

looked back to find him scowling at a roll of red ribbon. "What's wrong?"

"Nothing. This reminded me of something, that's all."

"A happy memory?"

"You could say that."

"Hmm. Care to elaborate?"

"It was those shoes you wore to the party last week. The red ones with the ribbon ties around the ankle."

I fell silent, riveted to the way he rubbed at the silk. There was something so controlled about the movement that had my pulse racing, even though I wasn't entirely sure why.

"I remember. Though I'm surprised you do too."

"They were very memorable." Rafe stepped right into my personal space, barely a breath between us. He looked down at me like I was his only focus, his eyes dark, hungry. "You know what else?"

"What?" I breathed out.

"Ever since I saw you wearing those heels, I've dreamed about tying your wrists with red silk. It has to be silk so it doesn't mark your skin. And then I'd stretch you out on the bed and tie you down, so I had free rein to do whatever I wanted to your body."

Oh.

My.

God.

My face heated to a thousand degrees.

I didn't move. Didn't blink. My breathing picked up a bit. "Rafe..."

"I've shocked you," he said, then he took the end of that silky ribbon and ran it along the edge of my jawline and across my parted lips.

I clamped my mouth shut and closed my eyes. Counted to five. All the numbers in existence weren't enough to dislodge the moment from my memory. "You don't know what you're saying right now. Go away before you say something else you'll regret."

"I rarely have regrets, Talia. But the ones I do have all seem to be linked with you."

There was that horrible pinch in my chest again. I snatched the ribbon back and threw it into the box with more force than necessary. "What does that even mean?"

"Do you really want to know?" he asked. "Sometimes I'm not sure you're ready for the answer. You ran away from me quick enough last week."

"What did you expect?"

"I expected us to talk like adults."

I couldn't argue with that and yet… I shook my head, throwing my gaze to the ceiling. "It's hard to talk to the person who rejected you. Tell me you understand that."

Rafe's lips pinched and his hands came up all clenched and splayed mid-air, like he wanted to reach for my head and shake some sense into me. "Oh my god, you drive me fucking crazy. I wasn't rejecting you. Did you know how much I had to restrain myself that night? All I wanted to do was fuck you against that wall and make you mine. But we were too exposed. I was trying to protect you."

Silence.

Pure adrenaline scorched my veins.

I'd replayed that night endlessly in the days since it happened. Retraced the sensation of his hands sliding up my thighs, wrenching my thong to one side so roughly, I'd been convinced he was going to rip the material and wouldn't have cared if he did. I'd almost told him as much at the time, except all my words had frozen in my throat the moment our mouths met.

He'd stunned me then as much as he stunned me now. But there was nowhere to run this time. No party to hide behind.

It was me and Rafe and silence for miles.

I stepped closer. One single step.

Rafe's eyes darkened with that potent mix of heat and intent, recognition. His nostrils flared as he took a few steadying breaths, like he was holding himself back. Hesitant at first, I rested my hand against his heart. His eyes closed the instant we touched, and it was that sign of sheer relief that soothed something in my mind and maybe my heart.

His groan caught in his throat as I reached for his neck and pulled his mouth down to mine. He gripped fiercely at my waist as our lips melted together and our tongues met in a slow, wet slide, and I was wrong earlier, so wrong, because I wouldn't think about anything but this.

CHAPTER 7

❄

RAFE

"So there's something I've been wondering about," Talia gasped out as we made our way up the hill. For a second there was nothing but the whistle of the wind and the crunch of our footsteps in the snow.

"Oh yeah, what's that?" I choked out around my own choppy breaths. I worked out five days a week and considered myself pretty fit, but the angle of this hill was deceiving from below.

My calves burned. My lungs ached.

The higher we climbed, the more I regretted my suggestion to sled down it using a twenty-five-year-old snow sledge I'd found in the garage. Not the best idea I'd had, but life at the moment was all about distraction when all I wanted to do was throw Talia on the bed and fuck her until she screamed. Until she was covered in me.

Who was I kidding? I didn't need a bed at this point.

It was going to happen. Talia knew it, I knew it. My dick did too.

It just hadn't happened yet.

I wasn't sure what we were waiting for, not after everything I said, after the kiss we shared the other day – and the mind melting kisses we'd shared since – but this needed to be on Talia's terms, so I was waiting.

She climbed a couple of steps ahead, the full, round curves of her ass right there in my line of sight, and I held back a groan.

I wasn't good at waiting, especially not when I'd decided on full steam ahead.

"Why is it called Chestnut Cottage?" she asked. "There's nothing remotely chestnutty about this place."

"Chestnutty," I mouthed, completely amused by her. She had a point though. There were no trees. Just miles of wide, rugged open land. "I think there used to be a chestnut tree here years ago. But don't quote me on that."

She paused for a second, swaying until she righted her balance. "I think this will do."

I blew against my hands and rubbed them together while I scanned the frozen landscape. From this perspective we could see all the way down the slope, past the cottage and the small loch further down the valley. The village sat further afield, a small cluster of grey rooftops and smoking chimneys. The only sign of life in days.

"I think we might've underestimated," I admitted, glaring at the route we'd climbed. "I don't remember it being this steep. We might pick up too much speed. I don't want you to break your damn neck, Talia."

"You're extra grumpy today." Talia nudged my shoulder with her chin and rested her cheek there. The closeness should have settled me, but I was a weak man right now. Right back on that edge. "It'll be fine," she reassured. "Unless you don't want to."

I didn't now I was up here, but I never backed down from a challenge. Not once.

"Let's do this."

I climbed into the sledge first and Talia followed, slotting herself into my lap, lodging that ass of hers right against my cock. Patience truly tested, I dropped my head against the back of hers for a moment, and she laughed. She knew exactly what she was doing.

"You ready?" I asked.

She let out a little *eeeeeeep* noise full of nerves and excitement. "Go, go, go, before I change my mind!"

I leaned back, gripping hold of the rein with one hand and pushing against the hill with the other to gain some forward momentum, and then we were off. The sledge picked up speed quickly, exactly as I'd feared, but Talia laughed and shrieked the whole time, and I would've done it again just to hear that sound. As we careened closer to the cottage, my heart disappeared somewhere to my throat, along with my balls probably. In a blink the gradient lessened and the ground dipped, and we soared, flying through the air – at least that's what it felt like – before landing and rolling, rolling, rolling, ending in a heap of snow only metres from the wall at the back of the garden.

Holy shit.

That was so close. Too close.

For a long time we were a breathless tangle of limbs; my left leg crossed with her right, my arm awkwardly crushed underneath her back. I spat and rolled my tongue. Some of her hair was in my mouth.

"Talia, are you okay?"

A giggle rang out, and she pushed up on her gloved hands, staring down at me with breathless joy. "That was amazing. I can't believe I sledded on Christmas Eve. This is a bucket list moment, Rafe."

"Yeah, a bucket we almost kicked."

"Stop it." She fell back laughing, like my grumpiness was

the funniest thing she'd seen all year, maybe delirious with adrenaline and the biting cold.

"Never again," I groaned, patting my chest which was thankfully still intact. Nothing hurt either. Also a good sign. "I'm too old for this shit."

She laughed harder.

"Hey!" I rolled her under me, my hips cradled by the warmth of her thighs. Her hair was in disarray, damp from the snow, and her cheeks and nose flushed the rosiest shade of pink. She grinned up at me and I grinned right back before smashing our lips together. The kiss was two seconds of slow and then minutes of hot, dirty thrusts against each other without any thought but chasing pleasure. So much pleasure.

If this is what it's like fully clothed...

Talia tugged at my hair, pulling me away from that lush mouth, all kiss-bitten and pink, and I blinked down at her in alarm, still drunk on her kiss.

"Take me to bed," she whispered desperately. "Take me to bed right now."

I would've taken her to the moon if she'd asked.

❄

We staggered into the cottage, tearing off our scarves and coats and working through multiple layers intended to keep us warm but massively inconvenient. I sent the coat rack flying with an, "ooops, shit, fuck," and Talia fumbled with the button on my jeans while I yanked at the zip on her fleece hoodie hard enough to rip it off. I stared at the metal in my hands for two bemused seconds and tossed it, forgetting its existence before it even hit the floor.

"I'll buy you a new one," I rushed out, peeling the hoodie from her shoulders along with her long sleeved thermal.

Talia loosened my jeans enough to slide her greedy hands right down the back, gripping the cheeks of my ass while I cupped her breast and my mouth found that smooth junction where her neck met her shoulder.

I bit down.

She whimpered.

She squeezed.

I moaned.

"I... I need to take my boots off," she said, warm breath grazing my skin.

"Let me."

I lifted her off her feet and set her ass on the coffee table. She wore nothing but a grey bra top and black leggings. She huffed a breathy laugh into her fist as I lifted her leg and swore and scowled through the zips and laces on her boots... how many fastenings did one boot need anyway? Talia struggled to contain that smile as I threw both behind me, shucked off my own shoes and stepped out of my jeans.

"I'm not doing this right if you're laughing," I said, ripping off her leggings until they turned inside out, and she was down to a pair of simple black underwear.

The second she was naked, I was going to lose it.

"I don't know. You're not doing it right if you're not, in my opinion."

"You want a clown in bed?"

She didn't expect that, blurting out another laugh around my name, contagious enough that I did the same. It was ridiculous how every smooth, controlled part of me had flown out the window. I was wrecked for this woman.

Impatience burned beneath my skin.

"Definitely no clowns, just... fun," she said, resting one hand behind her on the table and lifting the other to beckon me over with a curl of her finger in my direction.

And I went, like a moth to a flame.

My cock ached, pushing against my boxer briefs, and Talia bit her lip at the sight.

"What do you want?" I asked, standing between those perfect parted thighs, clenching my eyes closed when she leaned forward to first nose, then kiss the trail of dark hair leading down from my belly button. Her fingers feather-light, she traced the elastic of my briefs, and I held my breath for a second. Maybe two. She watched me watch her as she lowered the material, my cock springing up between us.

"You," she whispered, those big green eyes gutting me as much as the admission. "Just you."

She circled her hand around my shaft, and I groaned, giving myself a minute to sink into the incredible sensation. Cupping her jaw, I ran the pad of my thumb across her lips, not gentle about it either. Talia's tongue curled out to lick it and the desire I felt as I spread all that wetness over her lips was unmatched.

"God, look at you," I murmured, shaking my head in awe. So many times I'd imagined her like this, usually on her knees, but this visual – the reality – had that beat.

I swept up all that hair in my fist and guided her to my cock, her mouth the perfect height. Talia swirled her tongue around the head first, and my hips flexed. Heat speared down my spine. Easing into it, she suckled my flesh in slow, deliberate stokes, determined to drive me wild. But soon she was rolling her mouth down my entire length until she met the circle of her fist, and I rocked and surged into every lick, every suck, every stroke.

This was bliss.

Madness.

Although where was the line?

I'd promised to take her to bed but couldn't wait, not even for a handful of stairs. Reluctantly, I pulled my cock out of her mouth and ducked to kiss her there instead.

"You're perfect," I whispered, kissing her again.

I tugged her to her feet. The wet tip of my cock brushed her stomach as we stood there, so close but not close enough. I wanted to climb inside her skin somehow, burrow as deep as she was in mine.

Drawing her arms above her head, I whipped her bra top off, a stretchy scrap of fabric I never wanted to see again. Her breasts dropped slightly against her ribcage, and I traced the indent in her shoulder where the elastic had imprinted red on her skin. I kissed the spot gently and teased the full weight of her breast, running my thumb across her nipple.

"Rafe," she gasped.

"Wait till I get my mouth on you," I murmured, and saying it out loud had my cock hardening in anticipation.

Talia moaned, letting me lower her gently to the rug in front of the fireplace, lifting her hips to help as I tugged her underwear off.

And then there she was.

I didn't know where to look first. She was everything that drove me fucking wild. Full hips and thick, solid thighs, tits more than a handful with pink-tipped nipples ripe for my mouth. Every excuse I'd ever made to keep my distance evaporated from my mind.

I crawled over her, holding my weight with fists on either side of her head. "I'm gonna learn every fucking path of this beautiful body," I said roughly, and Talia's muscles spasmed in delight.

"Is that a promise?"

"A certainty."

I kissed her again, grinding against her pussy with enough pressure to tease but not nearly enough to get her off. She shifted her hips to match the movement of mine, her hands leaving trails of fire everywhere she touched.

Eventually, I pulled my mouth away and dotted kisses

down her neck, across her tits, along the little curving slope of her belly, all the way to where I'd wanted to bury my mouth last week.

"Touch me already," she whined, arching her body against me.

"Where?" I dragged one finger down her soaking wet pussy. "Here?"

Her body jerked and she parted her legs wider. "Harder. I won't break."

I did as she asked, shoving two fingers inside her, curling them in a come hither motion, and circling her clit with my thumb, adding extra pressure every time she made a noise that told me what she liked. Talia slapped against the floor, gripping the edge of the rug as I fucked her with my fingers, and I growled behind gritted teeth, electrified by the hot, wet sound.

It didn't take long for a shudder to roll through her, tossing her head to the side and letting out a soundless cry as she clamped down hard. When she came around, eyes lust-drunk and heavy lidded, she smiled but pushed my hand away, still shuddering from the sensitivity.

"I should have known you'd be good with your hands."

"I'm good with other things too," I said, and winked.

With a laugh she tugged me down to the floor and rolled me on to my back. "Let's see how good you are," she said, dropping in my lap and rocking herself back and forth over my erection.

The sight, the sensation, had me feeling wild, untethered somehow. Patience gone. I yanked at the drawer under the coffee table and fished out the condom I'd stashed inside the day before, more wishful thinking than planning ahead.

Talia's mouth lifted in amusement. "Look at you, a regular Boy Scout."

"Safety first," I joked, then lay back on the floor.

She shook her head with another laugh and snatched the condom, carefully opening the packet before rolling it down my cock. Shuffling forward on her knees, she positioned me exactly where she wanted and then—

"Fuck," I said desperately, taking a second to close my eyes.

Too much. Too much.

"Watch me," she demanded softly.

I opened my eyes. Riveted to the way she held my gaze as she slid up and down my length, inch by slow wet inch.

We both groaned.

Talia leaned forward, resting her hands on my chest to give herself more leverage as she slowly fucked herself on my cock, and I couldn't have taken my eyes off her if I tried.

I touched her everywhere I could reach – cupping her tits from below, pinching and pulling her nipples until they were red and she whined, rubbing that swollen clit with my thumb. Her skin was painted in firelight and shadows, and the sight of her like this, rolling her hips harder and faster, squeezing me so tight I could see stars, was enough to make me snap.

Grabbing her hips hard enough to bruise, I powered into her from below. Ferocious slaps over and over, again and again. The temperature rose and I could feel the pressure of my own release building and building from within, burning up my spine—

"I'm gonna come," Talia breathed out the moment she clenched around my cock, and all it took was that vicious wave and shudder, then I was coming too, pulse after pulse of agonising bliss.

At some point Talia slumped forward, panting against my chest, and I smoothed directionless patterns across her back dusted with sweat, my breaths lifting tufts of her hair as I came down from the high.

We lost time for a while.

Eventually, Talia climbed off me and collapsed onto her back while I removed the condom. We lay there side by side, nothing but the sound of the fire crackling next to us and the awareness that everything had changed.

I searched for her hand and weaved our fingers together, the action drawing our gazes in shock but also understanding.

Talia made a face that said *what now?* and I shrugged because I had no idea except that I wanted to do that again, as many times, and as soon as possible.

CHAPTER 8

❄

TALIA

THE SWEET SENSATION of fingers drifting along my hairline was the only way I wanted to wake up from now on. One fingertip took a soft detour to circle my ear and down the edge of my jaw. Rafe was learning every path of my body, just like he'd promised.

My mouth settled into a dozy grin.

"Morning," I said, voice croaky with sleep.

His fingers paused. I let my body tense in a quiet, gratifying stretch before hiding my smile beneath the covers. Last night had been incredible and I wanted to bask in it for as long as possible. If I'd been alone, I would've rolled around in the bed and clutched all the pillows while I squealed like a teenager after her first date.

I hadn't done that after *my* first date.

"Good morning," Rafe replied, tugging the sheets away and drawing my chin upwards so he could better see my face. I loved the way he held me, framing my throat like it was his to claim.

He could claim anything and everything, if he hadn't already.

I tried to fight him off, half-heartedly, and he rolled on top of me, tickling under my arm and down at my waist and that sensitive spot low on my hip that made my stomach clench.

He'd licked me there last night and I'd jerked just the same.

I laughed, wriggling about in the bed, our legs tangling beneath the covers, twisting up the sheets until they were an uncomfortable bunch beneath my spine.

Rafe peered down at me breathless and smiling, hips cradled between my thighs. I ran my fingertip between his brows, down the little line usually deep with a scowl, but it wasn't there this morning. I followed the path down his nose, over that tiny bump and—

"I fell down the slide."

"What?"

"I broke it when I was fifteen, walking down a slide in the park. Why are you smiling?"

I wrestled with my grin and the joy in my heart, but it was impossible to fight it. "I've always wanted to know."

"And now you do..." He ducked to kiss my lips, adding, "come with me."

"What?" I peeked at the radio alarm clock on the bedside table. "Ugh, why are you even awake, you monster."

"Don't act like you don't also get up at 4.30 every day."

"That's when I'm working. At Christmas? I won't hear of it. Anything before 8.00 a.m. doesn't exist." I gave his ass cheeks a satisfying squeeze, and right then I was grateful for squats. Grateful he did hundreds of them, grateful that I didn't. I wanted to rub myself off against all that hardened muscle. I could do it, too. I was sure. "Let's stay in bed."

Rafe rocked his hips in the most delicious tease and my breath caught. He was so hot it was ridiculous. "You're playing dirty, and I love it. But there's something I want to show you. We'll come back to bed, I promise."

"Fine," I said with a put-upon exaggerated sigh and threw off the sheet. "If you insist."

"Just shove some warm clothes on. Whatever is quickest."

"Okay." I frowned but did what I was told.

Once dressed, Rafe dragged me downstairs and told me to put on an old pair of his Wellington boots left permanently by the door while he grabbed the blanket still discarded on the floor from last night. He nudged me in front of him, my back to his front, and wrapped the blanket around the both of us until we were a warm, snuggly blanket burrito.

"What is happening?" I asked with a laugh.

"Trust me."

Somehow we managed to get outside without falling over each other's legs; the thick snow a crisp, satisfying crunch beneath our feet. I was so distracted by the sound, the fierce rush of cold against my cheeks, it took me a full minute to notice the snow floating around us in big, fat flakes.

Nothing around us but miles of white.

The sun hadn't fully risen yet but there was something ethereal, magical almost, in the way the dawn was so close, the air cold and still. Quiet. I lifted my face to the sky and, inexplicably, felt my eyes well with tears.

It was stupid, so stupid, but I couldn't help it.

My first ever white Christmas.

I was so used to the snow disappearing overnight or even an hour later back in London, I hadn't expected to wake up to… this. Even though it had been snowing for days. My brain hadn't allowed my heart to hope.

I'd never seen anything like it.

Rafe tightened his arms around me. I leaned my head

back against his chest and settled in to watch the snow dust everything like icing sugar.

I wasn't sure how long we stood there. After a while I turned around in the circle of his embrace, sliding my arms around his waist. Snowflakes dotted his hair and eyelashes, melting across his stubble, and the tip of his nose was pink with cold.

"This is perfect." I couldn't manage more than a whisper, the strength of my words lost to the intensity of his gaze. "Thank you."

"Merry Christmas," he said quietly, brushing my nose with his own.

The softness of the caress sent a shiver through my limbs and settled in my smile. "Merry Christmas."

❄

We were too wired to go back to bed. Rafe started the fire while I put on a cheesy Christmas movie that played every year on one of the main channels. It wasn't something I wanted to watch but the background noise reminded me of home.

After showering, I wrapped myself in the navy towelling robe I found hanging on the back of the bathroom door. The length of it brushed past my ankles, and the sleeves needed rolling up three times so I could see my hands, but it made me feel cosy and snug.

By the time I padded down the stairs in my thick wool socks, Rafe was setting out coffee and croissants on the coffee table, wearing nothing but a pair of grey sweatpants. His hair was slicked back, damp from our shower. I paused on the bottom step, unable to take my eyes off the V-shaped slope of his naked back. The faint red lines from my nails made the sight better somehow.

I'd been feral by that third round. Unhinged, probably.

"Is your back sore?" I asked, blushing lightly.

Rafe turned and smiled. His hungry eyes trailed the length of me, like he couldn't make up his mind where to look first, even though there wasn't anything to look at in this robe. I was cinched in at the waist but swamped in material.

"No," he said curiously. "Why?"

"You have some marks there now. Sorry."

I wasn't in the least bit sorry, but I was British. We apologised for everything.

Rafe inhaled so deeply his chest lifted considerably with the movement.

"You look mad," I said. "What did I say?"

"Nothing. It's just my face. I can't help it. If you must know, I'm trying not to rip off that robe, throw you down on the floor and fuck you until you scream."

The image was so vivid, everything tightened with arousal and throbbed between my thighs. I forced myself to take a breath, pulse racing, face too hot. "I'm not opposed to that."

He groaned, a gritty noise low in the back of his throat, fists clenched by his sides. "Get over here," he demanded roughly.

I rushed towards him, rocking up onto my tiptoes so I could reach his mouth, moaning at the feel of all his hardness wedged against my soft.

"I don't want you to hold back," I breathed out between hurried kisses. "Haven't we done that enough?"

"You have no idea what I want to do to you," Rafe gritted out. "No fucking idea."

Lost for words, I pulled on the ties at my waist and loosened the robe enough to expose a slither of my naked body. His nostrils flared as he drank me in. He ran one fingertip from the base of my neck, *down, down, down*, all the way to where I was hot and slick, needy for his touch. My legs widened, urging, begging for it, but instead he slid his hands inside the robe to grope at my hips and around to knead at the flesh of my behind.

"This ass… The things I want to do to it."

I whimpered. This was too much. He'd barely started, and it was too much.

"If you ask, I might let you," I whispered, and Rafe snapped.

He crushed our lips together again, a greedy lick into my mouth, kissing me so hard I grasped at his shoulders the way I needed to gasp for air. Desperate and needy. There was something near hysteria the way our tongues melted together hot and wet, and he yanked at the collar of the robe, so rough I thought it would rip.

The robe slipped from my shoulders, but the sound of my phone ringing on the coffee table startled us apart.

I glanced at the screen and whined. "I knew it. I just knew."

Rafe breathed against the slope of my shoulder, mouthing delicate kisses that belied the fierce grip he had on my waist. "You better answer it then."

"We're kind of in the middle of something here," I said, rubbing at the bulge in his sweatpants until he paused his torment to choke out a groan.

"Do it. She'll only keep ringing otherwise."

Ugh. Why did he have to make sense at a time like this?

"I… I can't think when you're touching me. Go stand over there."

Rafe laughed, giving my shoulder one last bite before I pushed him away.

"Hi, Mum," I managed, though I wasn't sure how. Every

cell in my body was on fire, alert, *primed*. I had to take a seat in case my knees gave out. "Merry Christmas."

"Merry Christmas, sweetheart. I missed you this morning."

"I missed you too," I lied. *Oh my god, I'm a terrible person.* I hadn't given anyone else a second thought when I woke this morning. The only person on my mind watched me from across the room like I was about to be his next meal.

To give him a taste, I parted the robe fully and opened my thighs, smiling when Rafe's eyes darkened.

"What will you be doing today?" Mum asked.

Climbing Rafe like a tree.

Getting bent over the sofa hopefully.

"Oh, you know, the usual. Watch Christmas movies and stuff my face. There will be alcohol involved too."

Maybe I'd let Rafe lick wine from my body. He liked wine and seemed to like my body, so it sounded like a great combination. Unconsciously, I traced the path the liquid would take as if he'd already tipped it down my chest.

Rafe clutched the back of the sofa, captivated by the trail of my fingers as I circled my breasts.

My nipples tightened.

I needed to get off the phone.

"Can you promise me you'll eat something other than chocolate, Talia?" Mum said, and I frowned trying to remember what we were even talking about. "If you were here you'd have something more substantial to line your stomach. I don't want you getting alcohol poisoning."

"Sometimes I swear you forget I'm thirty-five years old."

"You left us for Christmas. The least you could do is promise me this one thing."

"Fine. Fine. I'll eat a proper meal. I promise." *Christ.*

"Well, that's something at least."

Rafe rounded the sofa and without the back in the way I

had the perfect view of his thick, hard cock tenting the front of his sweatpants. *Thank god for light grey sweatpants.* I clenched my legs together, something, anything to alleviate the pulse between my thighs.

One touch, just one touch and I was going to come. I was sure of it.

"I'm also going to do some exercise," I confessed, trying not to sound too breathy, but it was so hard when he looked at me like that, the thick slab of his chest and abdomen right there for my greedy eyes.

Rafe's brow lifted curiously at the same time Mum said, "On Christmas? That doesn't sound like you."

"I know but I'm feeling… inspired."

"Right, well, as long as you're okay. You're not lonely?"

"Not at all," I squeaked out as one of Rafe's big hands circled my ankle and smoothed up the length of my calf, sending a rush of goosebumps in its wake. I clenched my eyes closed for a second. "I'll call you tomorrow. Send my love to everyone."

"You don't want to speak to your brothers?" Mum sounded aghast but that was the last thing I wanted to do.

"We prefer to text."

Rafe bought my leg up to his mouth, his breath warm against my skin, and I wasn't even sure what I was saying anymore.

"Okay then, darling. Have a nice day."

"You too. Happy Christmas, speak to you soon. Loveyoubye." I tossed the phone to the side somewhere. "I'm a terrible person."

Rafe chuckled against my leg and kissed my inner ankle. "Impossible."

"Take my socks off first," I said, intending to pick up where we left off.

He traced a fingertip along the elastic around my ankle. "Your feet might get cold."

"I don't care. Socks aren't sexy."

He laughed. "I disagree. You're wearing them."

"That was very smooth. Bullshit but smooth."

"I try," he said with a cheeky grin. "And it wasn't bullshit. Everything you do, everything about you is incredibly sexy to me."

My face warmed. Did he know the feeling was mutual, even though part of me wondered what had changed?

"Prove it," I whispered. *Challenged*.

Rafe's grin was slow to rise, like *just you wait*. He reached into his pocket, pulling out the roll of red ribbon, and my eyes blew wide.

❄

There was something wolfish in the way Rafe circled the bed, staring down at me with an expression hot enough to incinerate as I stretched out naked. I couldn't stop squirming as he removed two condoms from the bedside table and threw them next to me as if to say *you're in for it now*.

"How do you want me?" I asked, breathless with anticipation, my fingers knotted in the sheet, waiting, wondering what was going to happen next. I'd never been tied up before.

"Arms up," Rafe demanded, and I did what I was told. Some part of me always wanted to rebel, to push back and do the opposite, but right now all I could do was comply.

I was lost.

That should have unsettled me, but this was Rafe and that familiarity settled into my bones, easing my vulnerability. And I was vulnerable laid out like this, tied for someone else's mercy.

The bed frame wasn't conducive to tying me to it though,

nothing but a plain old headboard, and as if he'd heard my thoughts, Rafe admitted, "This would work better in my bed at home," almost annoyed he hadn't tried it there yet.

I hoped we'd get the chance.

Rafe crossed my wrists and looped the silk around them multiple times. "Look at me," he whispered, and ripped the ribbon with his teeth the moment I did, just like that. The ends freed allowed him to fasten a bow, loose enough that I could probably break free.

I didn't want to be free right now.

His hungry gaze swept down the length of my body. With my arms above my head, I was stretched taut, my back arched a little, thrusting my breasts higher on my chest. His breath grew heavy the longer he stared, and it was like an electric shock when he circled my nipple with the teasing tip of his finger, over and over again until they drew in hard and tight.

"This is torture," I gasped out with a whine.

"Not even close," he murmured, and replaced his finger with his mouth, swirling his tongue around my nipple and giving it a quick hard suck.

I panted, hungry for more.

I looked down at my chest and the sight of my nipple all red and wet with his kiss had my thighs clenching, a moan sifting out between my lips.

"You want more?" he said.

I nodded, adding, "So much more," as if the gesture wasn't enough.

Moving to the end of the bed, Rafe unravelled more ribbon and tied my ankles together in circles and loops of material. By the time he was done, my legs were tied together, my wrists positioned above my head, and my body was restless with want and need for whatever he had planned.

A throb sparked between my thighs.

Rafe gave me another blistering look as he shucked off his sweatpants, plucking a condom from the bed and rolling it down his hard length. He grabbed my ankles and yanked me to the end of the bed, my breath leaving me in a whoosh. A second later my bound legs were wrenched up onto his shoulder, and he paused to brush a soft kiss against my ankle bone, right above the line of silk. I watched him, breathless, as he positioned his cock at my entrance and slowly sank inside.

"Fuck," he breathed out, holding still and closing his eyes, one hand gripping my thigh – to anchor me or himself, I wasn't sure.

With my legs bound so closely, everything felt exquisitely tight and full, heightening the sensation of him surging inside. After twenty excruciating seconds, maybe more, Rafe looked down at me again, drawing out just enough before shoving back inside me with the kind of thrust that made my breasts bounce.

"Oh my god," I gasped, throwing my head back against the bed.

His eyes were glued to where he moved inside of me, mouth set with a snarl, and his thrusts picked up the pace, as if the sight electrified the action. Soon enough he was pounding into me and all I could do was lay there and take it, harder and deeper, whatever he wanted, whatever he tried.

"I need…" I choked out, body writhing right there on the edge, that tingly crest of a climax, so close and yet completely out of reach.

"What do you need, Talia? Tell me. Fucking tell me," he demanded roughly, hips pistoning back and forth.

I desperately wanted to touch him, needed to grip the muscle of his ass and feel it clench as he powered into me, and I struggled against the binding at my wrists.

"Touch me," I managed somehow. "Rub my clit."

A growl ripped from his chest, and he swept one hand up to my breasts, squeezing the weight, pinching my nipple, everywhere I hadn't begged for but somehow he knew I needed. My head rocked side to side and just when I was on the edge of begging for more, Rafe slid his fingers down to my pussy, teasing my swollen clit with soft touches and hard circles until I went out of my mind, overloaded with exquisite sensation.

My breath caught in my throat.

"Yes, come all over me," he said tightly. "Fuck."

My ass lifted inches off the bed as I clenched around his cock, an endless cycle of jerks and shudders until I was a wrung-out puddle of bliss with ringing in my ears. Rafe gripped me tighter, powering through my orgasm with deeper, wilder thrusts, over and over until he cried out and slumped in a breathless, sweaty mess.

I couldn't take it. I couldn't.

"Untie me," I begged. "Untie me right now."

Immediately Rafe snagged the ribbon and tugged it free. Concern flashed in his eyes until I threw my hands around his neck, smoothing them up to his jawline, touching him the way I needed. His gaze darted between mine, his expression softened. I pulled him down to my mouth and kissed him hungrily, hoping he heard everything I wasn't yet brave enough to say.

CHAPTER 9

❄

RAFE

BOXING DAY STARTED with the Johnson family tradition of hot chocolate with marshmallows and *Home Alone*. We planned on three rounds of Monopoly – the usual best out of three to decide the winner – but round two ended with Talia flat on her back on top of the board, fake money and game pieces scattered everywhere. It took ten minutes to find the little silver top hat while we settled on a draw.

Late afternoon we went for a walk and then dozed for over an hour. I wasn't sure if we both needed to catch up on years of lost sleep or if our bodies were finally relaxed enough not to fight it, but I'd never napped so much in my life.

When I woke, the bed was empty beside me, and Talia was padding around the bedroom barefoot, in nothing but one of my flannel checked shirts. A soft, dreamy smile played with her mouth as she re-rolled the length of red ribbon I'd thrown on the floor the night before. I stretched and clasped my hands behind my head and watched her move, eating up the sight of her smooth, solid thighs, my grin dark when she bent over.

I'd never tire of *that* view.

"What are you up to?"

Talia dropped the ribbon onto the dresser and whirled around. "Just tidying away. I thought you were asleep."

"I'm very much awake now." I winked, nodding at my cock tenting the sheet.

She laughed, sending me a look of faux shock. "A gift, for me?"

"Already unwrapped."

She shook her head softly, fingertips pressed against her smile. "But I didn't get you one. What can I get you?"

"How about you come up here and sit on my face. That'd be gift enough."

Talia's amusement vanished when she realised I was serious. After a second's pause, she slowly unbuttoned the shirt, teasing me with glimpses of her skin, the slope of her cleavage without a bra. The way the fabric slithered to the floor energised me like nothing else. I kicked the blankets and sheets to the end of the bed, not even ashamed I was quick about it.

Eager and painfully aroused, I patted the mattress next to my head. "Right here, baby."

Talia climbed onto the end of the bed and crawled up my body, pausing to kiss the dip of my hip bone. The shivery caress of her hair as it fell in her face and across my cock had me groaning, and she looked up the length of my body with a glint in her eye and a smug little grin. *Tease.* She swung one leg over my shoulder and took a bracing breath as she hovered above my face. There was a vulnerability shadowing her eyes, given the intimacy of the position, and the only thing that surprised me was that I was allowed to see it.

"Beautiful," I whispered, mesmerised by the obscene way she was spread out for me, the wet splay of her sex. She scraped her fingertips through my hair and across my scalp while I smoothed my hands up the outside of her thighs, over the wide crest of her hips and up to her breasts. Everything about her body lit me on fire, generous enough to grab and clutch and *squeeze*, and I did so over and over, starved for her even though it had only been hours since we'd last fucked.

Talia leaned into my touch as I lightly circled her areola once, twice, three times, before I gave her nipple a solid pinch and tug, nothing even remotely gentle about it. Her mouth dropped open, her head rolled. Signs of pleasure I'd imagined for so fucking long, but nothing came close to matching the real-life visual.

My cock was as hard as a fist.

I dropped my hands to her thighs again, kneading the flesh there, and tried tugging her closer.

"You sure?" Talia double-checked, still clutching the bed frame, bracing her body weight. "I'm not exactly light. I might suffocate you."

"Fuck, I hope you do."

"You asked for it," she said with a grin, and I wanted to shout *yes, yes I fucking did*, as she dropped her weight fully against me.

"Merry Christmas to me," I murmured, and Talia's spluttered laugh twisted into a throaty groan when I sank my tongue deep inside her.

"Fuck," she said breathily as I licked up the full length of her, circling her clit a few times before a hard suck made her whole body shudder. One hand still gripped the bed frame and the other clenched in my hair, directing me this way and that, telling me exactly what she liked without saying a word.

I groaned into the slickness of her, alternated with measured licks and sucks that made her lurch and grind, and I couldn't believe I got to see her like this, writhing senselessly against my goddamn face.

Talia reached back to grab my cock but there was no

finesse in the way she tried to stroke me, too lost to the need to clench down and ride.

"That's it, you're so fucking hot," I took a breath to murmur and slapped the outside of her ass, a loud thwack lost to the room.

"Rafe," she moaned, her voice more breath than sound, and I growled and gripped her thighs, lifting my head off the pillow to bury my mouth closer, deeper, mindless with want. Talia's hips rocked harder against the rumble of my moan, and she closed her eyes as she climbed higher and higher and—

"I'm coming," she choked out, her body as taut as a bow string before she broke and moaned and shuddered all over my face.

"How was that?" I asked, feeling pretty smug as I stroked her skin and pressed a slick, wet kiss right at the top of her thigh.

"I should be asking you," she panted. "It was your gift."

"Best present ever."

❄

With the room dimly lit by the fire's orange glow, we sat on cushions on the floor and picked at our dinner of cheese and crackers, chorizo, chutney, brown pickle and red grapes on the coffee table. Talia gave a little clap of delight at the spread and chewed on a few grapes while she filled her plate, and I couldn't help the smile crawling across my face.

Another incredible day. Despite the long walks and rounds of sex, my muscles were loose and limber. The headache that usually appeared every afternoon had been missing for a week now. I'd never been so content.

Thirty-nine years was a long time to go without this feeling.

"Did I ever tell you I bought this place from my parents?"

Talia glanced up from spooning dollops of caramelised chutney across wholewheat crackers and slices of cheddar cheese, pausing to lick her fingers, and I lost my train of thought. "Mrs Brown mentioned it," she said, her oversized sweater slipping down one shoulder.

"Of course she did." I chuckled, leaning over to kiss that smooth slope of uncovered skin. Needing to know everyone's business was probably the reason she hadn't retired. "Can't help herself."

"She also said that it's been in your family for over one hundred years," Talia admitted. "Why did they want to sell after all that time?"

"They thought the place was wasted sitting empty all year, which is true. But there's so much history here. Too much." I pointed at the rumpled angel perched at a sad angle on the tree, no matter how many times Talia made me adjust it; the fireplace garland that had seen better days twenty years ago. "Those decorations, they're from when I was a kid. I don't remember much but I do have some memories of spending Christmas here. They were mostly good ones too. I guess I wanted the reminder. Just in case."

"For your own family?" she asked tentatively.

"That was the dream."

"But not anymore?"

"I don't think dreams ever go away unless you make them a reality."

Talia nodded, seeming lost in thought. "Well, I'm glad you have some good Christmas memories at least."

"Not just some. I have a lot. Thanks to your family."

Her smile was brilliant and blinding and caught me right in the chest. "What changed, do you think? With your parents?"

"I don't know," I admitted with a one-shouldered shrug,

then topped up our glasses with red wine. I'd often wondered the same thing. "I grew up, I guess. Everything lost its magic when I stopped believing in Santa. Maybe the magic wore off for them too?"

"Maybe. It's sad though. But it's their loss, not yours."

I rarely discussed my parents. Rarely discussed anything unless it was a need-to-know basis. But it was obvious Talia and the rest of her family had their own impressions, and for some reason I needed to explain. "You know, my parents aren't bad people. If I'm being honest, they actually have the kind of relationship I'd like to have."

Talia blinked in shock. "Really? That surprises me."

"Why?"

"Because they act like you don't exist sometimes."

I winced. I understood, but they were still my parents. "It wasn't quite like that."

"You don't have to defend them."

"I'm not. I'm just telling you what it was like. My parents are the love of each other's lives. They're so wrapped up in each other that, yes, I was a bit like the third wheel. I suspect they had me because it was the expected thing. A box to tick maybe? Someone to take over the family business for them most likely. It happens."

"That makes it worse, Rafe," she said. "That's not a relationship to look up to. You don't have kids to tick a damn box. I hate that they've made you feel like that."

"Not that aspect of it. I know they've made plenty of mistakes as parents. But the commitment they have with each other. The devotion. That's never been a bad thing. I want that."

Talia carefully set the spoon against her plate, sitting back to give me her full attention. "I didn't realise you were such a romantic."

"With the right person I am. Or I could be. I want to be."

"I see," she murmured.

"Do you?"

She blinked, startled by the seriousness of my voice. It felt like forever before she answered, her gaze steady against mine. "I think I do."

❄

After dinner we settled on the sofa to watch TV. We went back and forth while I scrolled the listings, but Talia conceded that yes, *Die Hard* was a Christmas movie and yes, we could watch it, even though I didn't give her much choice.

She fell asleep halfway through.

A combination of the warmth and the wine left me feeling the same so I stretched out lengthways and tucked Talia in front of me, resting my chin on top of her head. The TV was more background noise than anything and Talia's body felt as heavy as my eyes as she succumbed to a deeper sleep. I brushed her hair back, tucking it behind one ear. I wasn't sure how long I stared at her or the flutter of her eyelids, the way she opened her mouth to inhale a couple of times, smacking her lips together before resettling again.

I could've studied her all night and it wouldn't have been time wasted.

The crackles from the fire dwindled and the heat dropped. It needed stoking, maybe an extra log, but I couldn't move, and it was too late to bother anyway. I switched off the TV, ushering silence into the room.

My gaze caught on the picture on the bookcase in the corner – my mum, dad and me, age four or five, proudly posing beside the snowman I'd spent hours crafting. My dad's Scott tartan scarf wrapped around its neck. The snapshot was clear but nothing else about that day stood out. Often left to my own devices, I'd been disappointed I'd had to build the snowman myself but so happy when they agreed to pose beside me, so much so the memory was a happier one.

On impulse, I grabbed my phone. They were five hours behind in Antigua.

Rafe: Hey, Dad. A day late but Merry Christmas.

To my surprise, I received a reply ten minutes later.

Dad: Merry Christmas. Your mother sends her love.

Rafe: Thanks. Send her mine too.

Rafe: Can I ask you a question?

Dad: Sure.

Rafe: How did you have it all? How did you have a life with Mum and a successful business?

Dad: Hard work. Balance is not easy. I also depended on a lot of people.

Rafe: Is this your way of saying I should listen to Henry more?

Dad: It wouldn't hurt.

Rafe: Maybe you could tell him to stop comparing everything I do to you.

Dad: You're the CEO now.

Rafe: Point taken. But if I am the CEO, you shouldn't be getting updates from him.

Dad: Point taken.

Dad: It's nice to hear from you. One year maybe you'll join us for Christmas.

His words caught me off guard. I frowned down at the screen.

Rafe: I didn't think you wanted me to.

Dad: You're our son.

Rafe: You never pushed for that. You never said anything.

Dad: You're also our adult son. You can do what you want. We also figured you were happier elsewhere. Some little blonde caught your eye maybe. You always did have a thing for blondes.

I glanced at Talia. She'd slept with damp hair the other

night so the strands were wavier than normal, a wild spread across my chest. Her hands were clasped underneath her chin, breaths soft and even. Something flipped, then flopped in my chest.

Rafe: You might be right. Night, Dad.

Dad: Night, son.

"Night, beautiful," I whispered, mouthing a kiss against all that hair, and closed my eyes.

CHAPTER 10

TALIA

"I THINK it's time I walked to the village," Rafe said a few days later, distracted by his iPad. He'd checked his work emails every morning, not that it bothered me. If I still had a job, I would've been doing the same, and I wasn't a CEO. *Yet.*

It was another way I appreciated our similarities. How seamlessly our worlds had entwined. I didn't want to get ahead of myself, but it was so easy to picture us together like this in the future, sitting at the table eating breakfast, drinking coffee in comfortable silence while Rafe worked on his iPad and I defeated another level on Homescapes or browsed expensive shoes I could no longer afford on Selfridges' website.

It was so nice.

Normal.

I'd been so busy I'd forgotten what that felt like.

"What for?" I slathered strawberry jam on my third slice of toast, looking up in time to see a flicker of irritation slither across Rafe's face. His phone had his attention this time.

It also wasn't the first time I'd seen that expression today.

"To see when the road might be cleared," he added. "No one seems to be answering my calls about it."

"Oh. I didn't realise you'd contacted someone."

"I've tried. If you're not careful, you could get snowed in up here for weeks, especially as no one uses this road except us. Sometimes the snow ploughs bypass us completely if they don't think anyone is here. Saves time, I guess."

I nodded, even though I didn't have a clue. It had been years since I'd seen a snow plough in London. "Wouldn't it be easier if we tried digging one of the cars out? There's a couple of snow shovels in the garage. It shouldn't take long with the two of us."

"I think it'll be quicker if I walk. It's only ten minutes."

I rolled my eyes. He sounded like Oliver when he'd told me he could run five miles in fifteen minutes. *Yeah right.* And pigs could fly.

"Fifteen minutes by car and that's if the roads are clear. It'll take forever walking in this weather. What's the rush?" We had a fully stocked fridge and pantry, and I wasn't flying back to London for another four days, though now I wondered if Rafe had different plans.

I hadn't considered that possibility, hadn't thought to ask. Questions about the future – about everything – had disappeared the moment we slept together. Nothing else had seemed important.

"Just getting things in order." Rafe snatched the slice of toast growing cold on my plate and crunched the crust, brushing at the crumbs caught in the knit of his navy sweater. "We have to go back to real life soon," he mumbled around the mouthful, then licked a blob of jam off his thumb.

Five minutes ago I would've grabbed his wrist and licked it for him, but my stomach was too busy sinking like an anchor, right to the soles of my feet.

Real life.

"Is this not real life?" I wondered out loud.

"Not really. Our lives are in London."

"Right." *Ouch.* I hadn't expected him to say that so easily, dismissively almost. Emotion burned thick in my throat, stinging at my eyes, and *don't cry, don't fucking cry, Talia.* "Of course. You must be busy."

"It's never-ending," he said with a sigh, scraping both hands down the sides of his face, rubbing circles at his temples. "Usually I'd delegate but I don't want to be the asshole calling my assistant a few days after Christmas, you know?"

"You're a great boss." I pushed my chair back, the noise stark in the otherwise quiet room, and started clearing the table. I dumped our plates in the sink, the cutlery a loud metallic scrape against the porcelain, and stared out of the kitchen window across the snowy landscape, willing my tear ducts to get their act together before I had to turn back around. "You should probably set off soon though, while it's still light. It won't be safe to go any later."

It was quiet for a long moment and for the first time since Rafe arrived, I hated the sound, the itch of it at my skin. I flipped the tap to fill the sink so there was some kind of noise.

"You're right," he said over the gurgle of running water. "I'll get changed."

My knuckles whitened as I gripped the edge of the sink, listening intently as he left the room, and only loosened my hold and all the tension in my spine once I heard the pad of his footsteps up the stairs.

Something had changed and it had nothing to do with clothes.

❄

Across the snow-dusted valley I could just about make out the back of Rafe's head as he walked toward the village. Despite the limited visibility, it was obvious there was still a lot of snow and probably ice on the road. My stomach knotted. One wrong move, that's all it would take, and I'd have no way of knowing if he'd been hurt and needed help. At best, a bruise or a broken bone. At worst... No. I couldn't bear thinking about it.

I needed to keep busy, keep moving. Watching TV or reading, any kind of activity that required sitting still, rarely helped. I cleaned the kitchen first before moving on to the bathrooms.

Over an hour passed.

I smelled like bleach.

Still nothing.

On my second pass through the kitchen, my gaze snagged on the village shop business card pinned to the fridge with a bottle opener magnet. I rolled my fingertips against the counter while I stared at it, deliberating. *Should I?* I shook my head, intending to walk away, but in the end I couldn't help myself. I needed to know. I dialled the number on the card, biting at my lip while it rang and rang.

"Oh my god, what?" a girl's voice said with sulky teenager tones.

Uh, hello to you too. "Is Mrs Brown there please?"

A loud, frustrated sigh bled down the line. Pretty sure I heard an eye roll too. "Hang on." There was a thunk, then a distant, "Nana! Someone on the phone for you!"

After a couple of minutes, Mrs Brown answered with a cheery and much more polite greeting.

"Hi, this is Talia. I'm staying at Rafe's cottage?"

"Oh, yes. Hello, dear. What can I do for you? Is everything alright?"

"I'm wondering if you've seen Rafe yet? He said he was

walking into the village to check the snow ploughs are coming?"

"Whatever would he do that for? The government deals with things like that."

I knew it. "Oh. Well, if and when you do see him, will you tell him to give me a call?"

"Of course, dear. I'll keep an eye out."

After our call I paced the living room, my mind filled with new questions, new fears. When the phone rang my shoulders sank in a combination of relief and annoyance, but only for a second. Leo was a master at texting but rarely called unless it was an emergency or if he needed to get out of an awkward date. The amount of times I'd had to pretend to be our mother was alarming.

"What's wrong?" I rushed out.

"Uh, hello to you too," Leo said, amused. "Nothing's wrong. I'm just checking in."

"You hardly ever call me though, unless you want something."

Silence filled the line. "Yeah, well, it's been weird not seeing you. No matter how busy things get at work, we always see each other at Christmas. It was strange, that's all."

"I know," I said with a sigh. I didn't regret my time spent away, not after everything that had happened, but it didn't stop the twinge of guilt. "I'm sorry I wasn't there."

"Hey, none of that. I understood the need to get away. Trust me. This isn't a guilt trip. I wanted you to know you were missed and to see if you were okay."

Aw. The fight eased its solid grip on my muscles and I sank into the armchair. Leo would walk through fire for me, for any of our siblings, but he rarely spoke his love and loyalty out loud. He was more actions than words, so this meant something. "That's sweet, Leo. I missed you guys too."

Even though I'd spent Christmas completely wrapped up

in Rafe and the way he touched me – the way he made me feel – I had missed my family and all our traditions. But it had also cemented how much I wanted someone special in my life. Family was one thing, but a life partner, someone by my side, was something else. I wanted it all.

I want Rafe.

I ached with want, desperate with it, especially now I knew what it was like to really, truly be with him. To wake in his arms and be wrapped in his embrace. No longer dreams or imaginings; I had actual memories now, solid moments I wouldn't be able to shake. I wasn't sure how I'd go back to before, wasn't sure if I'd need to. We needed to talk and now that Christmas had officially passed, it felt like we were running out of time. But maybe my uncertainty was warning enough? I should've felt more secure by now, after everything we'd shared, and yet…

Real life.

That's what Rafe said earlier.

Something seized in my chest. Was I even part of his real life? Did he want me to be?

"How was it?" I asked, desperate for distraction suddenly.

"It was fine. No tears," Leo joked. "Actually, it pretty much went as normal. Food, movies, presents. Dad pretended to be a good host while the neighbours stopped in for a sherry. Jacob cheated at Monopoly. Oliver fell asleep during *It's a Wonderful Life*. The usual. You didn't miss anything except the amazing present I got you, and my presence, of course."

I rolled my eyes but grinned at the picture he made. "Oh yeah? Well, I'll have something to look forward to when I get back. You can wow me with your presence then."

"You can count on it. I better have a good gift in return. Season of giving and all that."

"Guess you'll have to wait and see."

Leo chuckled. "Not too long I hope."

"Weather depending, I'll be home a few days after New Year's, I promise."

"But did you get what you needed? Has it been worth Mum's inevitable guilt trips?"

Yes. No matter if Rafe was about to break my heart completely, I couldn't find it in me to regret the time we'd spent together. Sometimes stolen moments were meant to be cherished, however fleeting.

"I think so." The urge to tell my brother what I'd decided about my career was right there on the tip of my tongue, but I held back for now. I needed to make sure I had the means to start my own business first. There was so much to do before I cemented things. "I have some things to work out but I'm getting there. Is… Is Dad still freaking out?"

"Nah. We calmed him down. He knows you'll be fine. Think he's mellowing in his old age."

I blew out a steady breath. One less thing to worry about at least. "Good. That's good."

"So you're really okay up there?" Leo asked.

"I'm fine. It's still freezing but the snow stopped finally. I got my white Christmas," I added with a fond smile. Standing on the front step that Christmas morning, wrapped in a blanket with Rafe while the snow drifted down around us was a moment I would never forget. The happiness had been all-consuming.

"So you and Rafe aren't trapped anymore?"

"Well, we can't get the cars out down the hill yet but… " My stomach lurched. "You knew he was here?"

"Of course, dummy. Mum wanted to know why he wasn't joining us for Christmas. He told us his plans."

But that meant my mum had known he was here when we last spoke on the phone. She'd never said a word. "His plans to…?"

"Go to the cottage with you? Yes."

"Well, he didn't exactly come with me. He arrived later."

"Tomato tomahto. Mum was thrilled. Word of warning, she might already be planning your wedding. We all wondered how long the two of you have been going on."

My brain blanked, long enough that Leo had to call my name to jolt me out of my silent stupor.

"I'm gonna shelve the whole wedding thing for later," I said calmly, even though my pulse had rocketed. "We were never on a romantic getaway. But for argument's sake, let's say we were. You're okay with it?"

"Why wouldn't I be?"

"I mean…" I circled my hand vacantly even though he couldn't see the gesture. "He's your best friend."

"And?"

I rolled my eyes to the ceiling. He wasn't getting it. "I'm telling you something happened between us and you're fine with it?"

"Again, why wouldn't I be? I'm not your keeper, you do whoever you want. That's your business."

I made a throaty noise of objection. "Try telling that to Danny Sheldon."

"Who?"

"My first ever boyfriend? You and Oliver terrified the shit out of him when he came to pick me up for a date and after that he refused to come to the house whenever you were home. Jacob once shot him right in the eye with his Nerf blaster and he had to wear an eye patch for over a week."

"Ohhhh, that snivelling turd. He was a loser. He doesn't count."

"But Rafe does?"

"I don't know," Leo said seriously. "You tell me."

My brothers knew exactly how to wind me up, but Leo had a particular knack for it. "Yes, he counts," I admitted with a huff.

"Good. What kind of shitty best friend would I be if I didn't think he was good enough for my sister? If there was anyone I'd be okay with, it's Rafe. He's one of the best guys I know."

My heart fluttered. "Leo…"

"Again, not that you need my approval or that he needs it. But you both have it, if that's important to you." The line went quiet, the pause as heavy as the lump in my throat. "Talia, have you been worrying about this?"

"YES. For ten years now. Probably longer. I don't know."

"Well, shit," Leo said, dumbfounded. "Why? That's stupid."

"I don't know!" I sounded as hysterical as I felt. "I thought there was some bro code or whatever. Anyway, if you're fine with it, why did Rafe take so long to tell me he likes me?"

I couldn't believe how much time we'd wasted. When I thought of all the things we could've done together already, my fists clenched painfully. There was nothing I despised more than wasted time.

"I don't know," Leo admitted. "I'm not a mind reader. It's Rafe. He's not exactly an open book. Maybe he didn't know you were interested? Because I have to admit, I had no clue you liked him. You kept that close to your chest. If I didn't know, how the hell was Rafe supposed to?"

Damn. It made sense when he put it like that. I was also a better actress than I realised. All this time I'd been convinced everyone could see it.

"I thought I had to hide it," I said, more to myself than anything. "I thought he didn't like me like that."

The regret shadowing his face after our drunken kiss haunted my dreams, even now.

"Well, maybe he felt the same way." Leo paused and then burst out laughing. "Can you imagine if you'd talked to each other years ago? You might be married with kids by now."

"Don't." Tears beaded at the corners of my eyes, the ache in my chest palpable. "I... I don't want to hear that."

"Talia, I... Shit. I'm sorry. I'm an asshole."

"No, you're not. It's just... It kills me to say it but in some ways Mum's right, you know? I don't know if you've ever worried about those sorts of things, but I have. It's something that's always there in the back of my mind. And right now, it hurts that maybe I could've had everything I've ever wanted if I'd been open about things. If we'd both been open about things."

If only I'd been brave...

"I'm sorry," Leo said, and the genuine note in his voice made the ache harder.

"It's fine. I'm feeling sorry for myself, that's all. I'll be okay."

"Maybe you can still have all of those things. It's not too late."

"Maybe," I said, shaking my head at myself and everything.

Leo was quiet for a long moment, whether to absorb the conversation or give me time to do so, I didn't know. "Technically, it's still Christmas and you're not supposed to cry at Christmas, remember?"

I sniffled and huffed out a croaky, wet-sounding laugh. Our mum would never stand for tears at this time of year, even if our hearts were breaking. "You're right."

"How about we change the subject, huh? Talking about your love life bores me to tears anyway."

"Wait until it's your love life, then we'll talk."

"Hah! I'm forty years old. That ship has sailed."

"What? That has to be the dumbest thing I've ever heard you say. You make it sound like you're eighty. Don't be daft."

"I'm happy as I am. Not everyone settles down. I'm fine with it."

"I know. And not to be all Mum about it, but part of me would like you to have someone to share your life with, as long as it makes you happy. Is that so bad?"

"No, it's sweet. You're sweet. Even if I wanna wring your neck sometimes."

"Well, now you ruined this lovely brother-sister conversation we were having. Goodbye."

Leo chuckled. "You know I just want you to be happy too, right?"

"I know."

"Stay safe, okay?"

"I will. There's not really much trouble I can get in up here anyway."

"For fuck's sake, Talia, don't jinx it."

"Bye!"

I laughed as I hung up and smiled at the phone until the screen darkened. Still nothing from Rafe. All I could do now was wait. And maybe when he returned, I would finally be brave.

CHAPTER 11

TALIA

The light had shifted to the other side of the cottage and Rafe still wasn't back. There was nothing more to clean and no messages to check so I decided to burn off my anxiety with exercise. Since jumping jacks hurt my boobs, I threw on my coat, two pairs of woollen socks and Rafe's old Wellington boots and stomped outside to dig out the cars.

Every scrape and forceful shove into the snow was another unanswered question.

Why did he lie?

Was it just convenient sex?

Is he okay?

Am I overreacting?

By the time Rafe appeared, my hands were stiff and frozen, my muscles ached, and the driveway was framed with mounds of snow where I'd started clearing a car-wide path.

Anger and anxiety were amazing fuel, as it turned out.

"Talia!" Rafe called out, gingerly jogging up the drive. About halfway, he threw his arms out to steady himself when his boot caught on a patch of ice, but recovered pretty smoothly. "What the hell are you doing?"

"What does it look like?" I gasped out between breaths. Worry melted to relief that he was okay, but I felt incredibly tired all of a sudden. I rubbed at the twinge blooming in my lower back and winced at the pops and clicks as my spine realigned after being hunched over for so long.

"Give me that," he said, motioning at the shovel. "You've done enough. The rest can wait."

"I'm on a roll now."

"You look like you're about to pass out. It's too cold for this." He drifted closer and tugged my chin upwards. "For fuck's sake, your lips are blue! Get inside."

"I thought I told you not to tell me what to do."

Rafe stilled, glancing around uncertainly. "What's going on?"

"I'm trying to clear the drive and you're getting in my way."

His mouth tightened. "Enough. Get inside."

"I'm not finished."

"Well, I am. I'm too cold and tired for this temper tantrum, Talia. Inside. Now."

"Excuse me?" Fuck the cold, my temperature surged to a million degrees. Even if he was right. Even if I was pushing the limits of bratty behaviour. I couldn't help myself. "Temper tantrum?"

He tore the shovel from my hands and threw it over the wall where it landed with a thud in the front garden. "Get inside or I'm carrying you in there. Your choice."

"Yeah, right. I'd like to see you try."

His eyes flared. *Shit.* Rafe loved nothing more than a challenge.

"You asked for it," he said, grabbing me around the waist and hoisting me over his shoulder.

I shrieked as the world tilted.

It took a fierce slap against my ass for me to remember how to use words.

"Put me down!"

"Nope."

"Seriously, stop." I clawed at the back of his coat, unsteady and off-balance despite knowing he'd never drop me. "You could hurt yourself!"

"Don't insult me," Rafe scoffed, shouldering open the door. He stomped out the snow on the mat and marched inside, throwing me down on the sofa. I gazed up at him in breathless disbelief as he shook his head and spun away, settling his fists on his hip while he seemingly tried to rein in his anger.

Did that just happen?

"What are you playing at?" he said finally, his gaze furious against mine. "You could catch your death out there."

The cushions scattered as I struggled up onto my elbows, too low and vulnerable all splayed out. "Oh, so you can disappear for half the day in the freezing cold, but if I spend a few hours out there, it's bad?"

"You've been out there for how long?" he demanded.

"It doesn't matter. What's done is done."

"Talia, what the fuck is going on?"

"You tell me. Where the hell have you been?"

"You know where I've been," he said, confused.

Right. So that's how he was going to play it. Fine. Somehow, I managed to climb to my feet, weary for more reasons than I could count and so not in the mood for someone to lie to my face. "I'm gonna take a shower."

Rafe stepped closer, face marred with a frown. "Talia."

I shook my head as if that was some kind of answer, too confused by the whiplash of emotions. How did the day start so wonderfully and end like this?

"We can warm up together?" he tried, a tentative tug at the zipper on my coat.

"I'm tired. We'll talk later."

Cupping my cheek, Rafe brushed his thumb across my cheekbone. "I know I was gone a long time. I'm sorry if I worried you. It wasn't my intention."

With a nod I headed for the stairs, too scared to speak around the lump in my throat and the fear I might start blubbering, and then where would I be?

❄

Freshly showered and changed, and warmer than an hour previously, I made dinner by heating up some tomato soup and serving it with crunchy wholemeal rolls. I didn't have the energy for anything more. Rafe leaned against the kitchen door frame, arms folded, watching my every move but didn't argue. Didn't say much of anything. Just leaned and scowled. His factory setting.

We ate in silence.

The contrast to this morning made my heart ache.

"So," I said at the same time Rafe's spoon clattered against his empty bowl.

"Are you ever going to tell me what's wrong?" he said.

I didn't know where to start.

Bravery was easier said than done now the moment had arrived. Every aspect of my life had fallen apart – or felt like it – in recent weeks and I'd somehow, inexplicably, managed to carve out this little space of joy. I couldn't bear the thought of losing it.

Losing him.

"I could say the same thing to you."

"What?" The genuine confusion furrowing his brow brought my brain to a halt.

Have I got this all wrong?

"You were acting weird at breakfast."

"You said you didn't mind if I checked my emails," he said, still puzzled.

"I don't. It's not about the emails. It's about you making up some excuse to walk all those miles in the freezing cold as if you couldn't wait to get out of here."

"It wasn't like that." Rafe scraped down the side of his jaw, the stubble a sandpapery noise against his palm. "I just needed some space."

"From me."

God, I hated how vulnerable I sounded.

"Of course not." He reached for me across the table. I wasn't in the mood to be affectionate, but it was instinct now and I let our fingers entwine, momentarily soothed by the hypnotic brush of his thumb. "Alan Fraiser pulled out of our deal. I found out this morning."

I clutched his hand tightly. "I'm so sorry. Why didn't you tell me? I would've understood if you needed some space. I need space too sometimes. I mean, it's the reason I'm here."

"I don't find sharing so easy, Talia. It's not my first instinct. But then it's not yours either, is it? You've been anxious about this all day and haven't said a word. It goes both ways."

"You're right. But you're not the one who was rejected the first time. You disappeared for hours today. I guess part of me is still waiting for the other shoe to drop. Again."

Rafe clenched his eyes closed for a second. "I'm sorry. I didn't think. Henry's blaming me instead of realising that Alan didn't want to sell in the first place. Some things don't have a price. His email pissed me off and I didn't want my mood to rub off on you either. I needed to get out and clear my head a bit. I should have told you though, and I'm sorry I didn't."

I nodded absentmindedly, absorbing it all. "So you don't want to leave?" I asked tentatively.

"Well, maybe not today, but I have to leave soon. There's only so much I can do from here."

My stomach dropped.

"I know that but I don't get the rush. Why do you want to leave so soon?"

"It's not that I want to leave. I have to." He frowned, watching me closely. "But the more important question is, why do you want to stay? If I didn't know any better, you sound frightened but that's not like you."

"Frightened?" My laughter rang out awkward and forced. "Don't be silly."

Adrenaline surged beneath my skin, making me itchy with it, restless. Needing to keep my hands occupied, I shoved my chair back so quickly it rocked on its feet. I drifted over to the sofa in the living room and pulled at the blanket hanging over the back. Once I'd shaken it out and refolded it again, I grabbed a cushion, punching and fluffing the stuffing over and over. Rafe snatched it out of my hands and tossed it on the floor.

"Talia, tell me. It's okay," he promised, fingers gently circling my wrist, but it was too soft of a gesture, too caring, too much somehow.

I pulled away, stuttering back a couple of steps. "It's not.

"Talia," Rafe said, more forceful now, more *cut this shit out*. "Please. We can't sort this out if we don't talk about it."

"That's rich."

"I know. But please tell me what's wrong."

"Everything!" I shouted, sudden enough that his eyes widened. I gestured helplessly at nothing and everything, hoping he understood, hoping it made sense. "Because it'll change. The moment we leave it'll be over. This. Us. I'll have to go back to making terrifying business plans and worrying about the future and pretending I don't know how it feels when you're inside me. How it feels to wake up with you by my side. Maybe you're fine with that. Maybe you can pretend, but I can't."

Rafe watched me intently, his breathing heavy. "Who said anything about pretending?"

"You said this isn't real life. I get it. I mean, my heart doesn't get it. But my brain? Yeah, I think I understand."

"Your heart?" he repeated softly.

I scrunched my eyes closed, slapping both hands over my face for a second. "Yes, I know, okay. I'm... This is embarrassing."

Rafe tugged my hands away and clasped my face between his palms. The fierceness of his expression caught me off guard and I rooted to the spot, unable to do anything but look up at him.

"Talia, listen to me. This morning, what I said... I didn't mean *we* aren't real life. Me and you, that's the realest part of my life in a long time."

My heart was in my throat. I was certain Rafe could feel the erratic race of it beneath his fingertips. "Oh."

"I meant this situation isn't real. We don't live in a remote cottage hidden away from the world, and we never will. Not permanently at least. I've got my business and you'll have yours one day and—"

"You really believe that?"

"Of course I do. You're incredible. You can do anything you set your mind to and when your heart is in it too? You're unstoppable."

Tears stung my eyes, beading at the corners enough that I had no choice but to blink them away, let them bleed down my cheeks and the tips of his fingers. I hadn't realised what it would feel like to have someone believe in me that much.

"Thank you," I choked out, clutching at the front of his sweater.

"This time with you here, the two of us, I wouldn't change for the world," Rafe confessed, brushing my tears away with his thumbs. "I needed this. We needed this. To see what we could be. This has been a long time coming. But our real life is in London, and that means being together around our family and friends and balancing all of that around work. That's what I meant."

I was too overwhelmed to say anything but, "Okay."

"Does that sound like something you would be interested in?"

I swallowed around the lump lodged in my throat and nodded, finally managing a smile. "Where do I sign up?"

Rafe grinned and my heart soared. His eyes lit up like I'd given him the greatest gift imaginable – *me* – but oh, that didn't seem possible. He ducked to even up our mismatched heights and we stood there, foreheads pressed together in joint relief. I closed my eyes, let out a breath, and sank against him.

"That's good to know," he murmured. "And maybe after our busy days you could come home to me and tell me all about your day while I rub your feet. I know how much you like your heels."

I drew back to look at him, elation stretching into my eyes. My cheeks ached with it. "I love my heels. I'm told they make my ass look fabulous."

"They really do."

"You noticed that, huh?"

"I noticed everything, Talia. Every single thing about you. I'm obsessed with you."

Exhilarated. That was this floaty feeling, right? This tingly rush of joy in my veins?

"Why did you never tell me?" I wondered. "Why push me away after we kissed all those years ago?"

"I don't know where to start," he said with sigh.

"Was it Leo?" I asked. "Because I spoke to him earlier. I didn't tell him anything, but he already knew and he was fine."

"I know. I told him I was coming up here. I mean, it was a worry in the back of my mind in those early days. I've never had a friend like Leo before. And then your family…" Rafe shook his head slowly, as if he couldn't quite find the words. "Your family accepted me as one of their own and that meant everything to me. You know what my parents are like. I've never had the kind of family life you and your brothers have had, and I liked that I was suddenly a part of it. And then there was my job. It takes over my life sometimes. When we kissed that first time, I'd only recently taken over as CEO and everything was so unsettled and chaotic, and I was always worried I'd never be able to give you the time you deserve. That's why I held back. It was never about Leo. Not really. There was just so much more to lose. I had to be sure."

I slid my hands up his torso, clasping them together behind his neck, and stretched up on tiptoe to plant a soft kiss to his lips. Just a little one, a taste.

"And you're sure now?" I asked. "You want to be with me for real?"

"I am with you for real. This hasn't been pretend. I need you to know that. How I feel about you, how you make me feel, is the most honest I've ever been. I love you."

Something swooped in my chest. My eyes widened. "What?"

"I love you, more than I could ever say." He shook his head in disbelief, a wry smile decorating his face. "Isn't it obvious?"

"I've spent the day freaking out so… not really, no."

Rafe huffed a laugh, tucking an errant wave behind my ear. "You remember you asked me why I told everyone you were my girlfriend?"

I nodded. Like I'd ever forget.

"The truth is, your name didn't just pop into my head. Your name is a constant. There is never a day I don't think about you in some way. Wondering where you are, what you're doing, who you're with. If you're happy, even if it was another man making you smile. You were – you *are* – always on my mind. Always, Talia."

"Rafe—"

"When someone asked if I was bringing anyone special to a work event, your name came out because of course it did. I didn't think you'd find out and it was nice to pretend. It was like it was real. You and me."

"Rafe," I begged, bouncing gently on my feet. "Please stop talking and kiss me already."

"I will but I need to know that you understand. That you trust in what I'm saying to you. That it's you and me from here on out."

"I do, I do understand. Now show me. Don't stop showing me."

Rafe grabbed my face, whispered something I couldn't decipher, and captured my mouth in a passionate kiss. Our tongues slid together, slow and wet, and the sexy hum in the back of his throat sent a zip and zing of pleasure right through my core. I must've made some sort of sound in response, too mindless to be sure, and he groaned, lifting me, pressing our bodies close.

I was a desperate, clinging mess of arms around his shoulders and legs around his hips as I nipped at his ear, and he squeezed my ass cheeks hard enough to leave a mark.

Our hands, everywhere, all at once.

My underwear, soaked.

I wasn't sure where he was taking me until I hit the back of the sofa. He perched me there while he teased the spot behind my ear, ran the tip of his nose all the way down my neck, peppering the path with kisses and soft bites, but I wanted more. I wanted everything.

"I'm out of my mind for you," he whispered against my clavicle, an echo of my own thoughts, dotting kisses down the deep V of my oversized sweater. He tugged at the neckline, pulling at the wool rough enough to stretch.

"This fucking thing," he whined, his voice a desperate throaty sound that made my thighs clench. "Take it off. Take everything off."

I did what I was told.

Soon enough our clothes were strewn across the living room, our naked skin lit by the fire behind. I gripped his shaft, circling the wet tip with my thumb, and he groaned, a deep rumble like it was ripped from his chest. He let me tease him for a minute or two, slow steady strokes up and down, needy whispers of *harder* and *more*, then he was cupping my breasts, closing his teeth around one nipple and then the other, driving me wild and senseless with sensation.

I ran my foot up the back of his calf and he jerked like a live wire, then somehow, I was flipped around to face the fire, barely catching my breath as one large hand pushed down on my back until I was bent over the sofa, ass thrust in the air.

"Rafe…"

I gripped the cushions, moaning in delight as he scattered my back with kisses, licked a line right down the arch of my spine to the crease of my ass. I didn't have time to think when he knelt behind me, a hungry groan rumbling from his chest as he spread me apart and licked right up the length, from the swollen flesh of my clit to where I was clenching around nothing, desperate to be filled. Words spilled from my mouth, *harder, lick my pussy,* spurring him on with rough and eager sucking at my clit, working his tongue up and down until I was a wet, writhing mess all over his face.

"Yes," I groaned. "Keep doing that."

"I can't," he whispered roughly, rising to his feet. "I can't wait."

Poised at my centre, I had seconds to prepare before he anchored one hand in my hair and his hips surged forward. One single solid thrust. He held still to choke out a groan, then it was nothing but sweet, mindless bliss as he pounded into me, over and over, again and again with hot hard slaps of *take it, just like that,* until we both broke and shuddered, crying out in a mix of relief and release.

Later, I laid out on the sofa covered only with the tartan blanket, my smile probably smug and definitely satisfied. I watched the muscles of Rafe's naked body clench and contract while he reloaded the fire with more logs and stoked the flame to a roaring crackle again. Every inch of his skin turned golden by the warm glow. The lights on the tree were static tonight. Calming.

When he was finished, he tucked me under his arm and mouthed a couple of kisses along my hairline, though the blanket barely covered us both.

"Did I ever tell you that I love you?" I murmured sleepily, my body lax and content.

"I think I'd remember you telling me something like that."

"Well, I do." I pulled back to see his reaction, traced his mouth as it widened with a smile and stretched slowly into his eyes. "More than I can ever say."

"That's my line, Sunshine."

"I didn't think you'd mind."

"Say it again."

Happiness bubbled up inside me again, almost too much

for my body to contain, and I fought the childish urge to wriggle in my seat. "I love you."

"I love you too." Rafe ripped the blanket away, tossing it somewhere into another realm as far as I was concerned, and pushed me back down on the sofa. He climbed between the cradle of my thighs, pressing our bodies close until I wasn't sure where we ended or began. "I better get to work on showing you how much."

EPILOGUE

RAFE

ONE YEAR LATER

Call me ASAP.

Rolling my eyes at the text on the screen, I switched off my phone and tucked it back inside my jacket pocket. Henry would have to wait this time.

"So how do you know Talia? Are you a client too?"

I paused in taking a sip of whiskey and shook my head at the grey-haired man leaning against the bar. I think he mentioned his name was David, but I'd been too busy staring at Talia laughing across the room so wasn't one hundred per cent sure. Unfortunately for David – that was his name now – Talia had cut her hair last week, some short wavy style, ending an inch past her chin, and I'd been distracted by the sight of her bare neck ever since.

I wanted to curl my hand around the back of it and pull her mouth to mine…

"No, she's my girlfriend," I admitted, though I hated that word. *Girlfriend.* It barely scratched the surface of my feelings and didn't fully encompass her importance as *the* woman in my life.

I hoped to change that soon.

"Well, you must be very proud," David said. "I have to admit we were a bit hesitant to work with such a new firm but she's exceeded our expectations so far. We've already noticed an uptick in sales based on our new social media directives. My wife is thrilled."

My chest warmed with pride, and I didn't even try to hold back a smile. Talia was the love of my life, and that put her on a whole other level to everyone else, but she was also my friend. I'd seen all of her ups and downs, or at least heard about them through Leo, especially in those early years. She deserved everything good that came her way, and I would've thought the same even if nothing had ever happened between us.

I didn't like to think about that alternative now. I felt nothing but dread whenever my brain tried to play a game of *what if?*

We're together now and that's all that matters.

"I'm glad to hear that," I said. "I know I'm biased, but I also know good business. Talia won't let you down."

David turned to study me properly, recognition settling on his face a few seconds later. "Of course. You're Rafe Scott. I know my business too," he added with a wink and a couple of taps against the side of his nose.

My grin deepened. I supposed that was true. Unless you were deep in the hotel corporate world or you'd read the interview I'd done in The Economist magazine a couple of years ago, very few people knew me by name. Just the way I liked it.

"Anyway, congratulations to your other half once again." He collected a glass of merlot from the barman, threw down a ten-pound note, and tipped the drink in a gesture of cheers.

"If you'll excuse me, I must rescue everyone from the horror of my wife's drunk dancing. I'm hoping this will tempt her off the dance floor. A little tip for the future: bribery works."

"Good to know," I said with a laugh. "And good luck. Enjoy your night."

David disappeared onto the makeshift dance floor, laughing when his wife threw her arms around his neck trying to get him to dance. As predicted, it wasn't until he offered her the glass of wine that she staggered away to a nearby table, clutching his arm, too wobbly on her own feet.

I shook my head in amusement and let my gaze circle the room. The lights had dimmed about half an hour ago and everything glowed red from the Christmas tree in the window, but I found her immediately.

Always will.

She had me spellbound. There was no other word for this… yearning that held me captive, riveted to her every move. Talia weaved around high-top tables and tall-backed leather chairs, stopping every so often to talk to someone, embracing everyone with her warm presence. A laugh, a quick chat, a hug. It didn't matter. She was the sun and they were all sunflowers reaching out in her direction.

I was the tallest of them all.

I remembered the last time I watched her work a crowd a year ago, at my own company Christmas party. The night she'd forever shifted my foundations. She'd put everyone at ease with a smile or a question that sounded like she gave a shit about the answer. There was no faking it, even though our relationship had been exactly that back then.

Thank fuck it wasn't now.

Last time she'd worn a slinky red dress forever etched on my memory, but tonight it was dark green – *forest*, like the trees, according to Talia – and stretched snuggly over her hips and ass. More than once I'd thought about tracing the criss-cross pattern of straps down the curve of her spine with my fingertips, maybe even my tongue, making her shiver because she liked that, feeling the heat of my breath against her skin as I discovered her body for the thousandth time.

Mostly though, I couldn't take my eyes off the swish and sway of silk around her legs. Every now and then I'd catch a glimpse of a pencil-thin heel and it made me so fucking hard that I was the only one who knew about the gold straps climbing the length of her calf. She'd been perched on the edge of our bed with me on my knees as I'd wound them up her legs myself, all the while making plans to fuck her later while she wore those heels and nothing else. *Fuck.* If I didn't get my hands on her soon, I might actually break something.

I drained the rest of my whiskey and set my glass on the bar. Better safe than sorry.

Ellie, Talia's friend and first ever employee, paused their conversation to point at me with a knowing smile, and Talia looked over her shoulder. *Finally.* Our gazes clashed with heat and purpose, because I'd told her, whispered not even two hours ago when we'd first walked into the room, that the moment our eyes met again she'd be mine and not even her company's first ever Christmas party would stop it. Professionalism be damned. Her mouth, painted a rich red I'd like to see circling my cock, quirked in a flirty grin, and I was going to destroy that later. Wreck her composure the way she always wrecked mine.

Talia's attention snagged on something over my shoulder, and the joy in her eyes faded as quickly as her smile. I turned to see what had stolen her fire, frowning at the raven-haired woman marching across the room. She had spiteful eyes, a jawline as sharp as a knife, and an air about her that screamed *touch me and die*. I had no idea who she was, but she'd erased the happiness from my woman's eyes and that wasn't fucking happening. Not tonight.

I intercepted her before she passed. "Hi. Rafe Scott. I don't think we've met?"

The woman slowly looked me up and down, her upper lip curled in distaste, and I blinked a few times. No one had ever looked at me like that.

"You're right," she said, refusing to shake my hand. "We haven't met."

Well then...

She'd barely taken a step away when Talia reached my side. "Nadia," she said. "I don't remember sending you an invite."

Nadia. My eyes widened and I clutched Talia closer. She settled her hand on top of mine, reassurance for my sake or her own, I wasn't sure. But I let her give or take whatever she needed, as long as she knew I was by her side.

"As if I need an invitation anywhere, darling," Nadia said snidely. "I taught you that."

"You did. I always thought it was rude though."

Her lips pursed, something cold and aloof in the way she glanced around the room, feigning interest. How Talia had worked with this woman for ten years, I'd never know.

"You don't get anywhere in this business being sunshine and flowers and polite hellos," Nadia said, rolling her eyes.

Sunshine.

Talia met my smile with one of her own. "But it sounds so nice and friendly."

"Friendliness gets you nowhere."

"Agree to disagree. Anyway, what are you doing here? It's not like you to check out the competition. How strange."

Throwing her head back, Nadia barked out a stilted, fake-sounding laugh. "Competition? Hardly. You're a speck on the horizon, darling. A particle of dust. I'll sweep you away soon enough."

"Right. Well, good luck with that." Talia grinned brightly. "While you're here you should go say hi to some of your ex-employees. There's a few of your old clients running around too. We're so happy to have them."

"As if I'd waste my time. Good luck, Talia. Clearly you're going to need it." With one last spiteful glare, Nadia tutted under her breath and whirled away.

"Oh. Was it something I said?" Talia asked with a laugh.

I bit back a growl at the punch of pure arousal and spun Talia around, earning a breathless giggle of delight. I lodged myself right up against her ass, curling my arms around her waist. She tilted her head enough for me to fit my chin in the crook of her neck, sliding her hands on top of my own, and we swayed slightly, tucked in our own little world.

"That was hot."

Talia rocked her ass against me. "That got you going?"

"It did," I said gruffly, nosing the ticklish spot behind her ear. "Not even ashamed to admit it. You're incredible."

"It felt pretty good."

"I bet it did." I shifted closer, letting her feel exactly what she was doing to me. "This feels pretty good too."

"Mmm." She rocked again, barely, but enough to make me groan. "I've imagined so many different scenarios if I ever saw her again but none of them matched the rush that gave me."

"She must be worried."

"Nadia Thomas doesn't worry about anything. She's more intrigued than anything. Maybe a bit annoyed I stole a few of her employees and clients. Well, technically they were my clients and happy to leave but semantics. She probably hated that."

"I don't know. I think if you were only curious you'd send

someone else to have a look around and report back, but she wanted to see with her own eyes. I know what a terrified business owner looks like and she had all the hallmarks of one. Harder to decipher than usual but the signs were there."

"If you say so." Talia spun to face me, draping her arms over my shoulders. "I don't care anymore. I feel as high as anything."

"Yeah? You happy?"

She nodded, running her fingers down my nose and the side of my face, and I ducked to kiss the inside of her wrist, inhaling the sweet, lingering scent of her perfume. No one else had ever treated me with such tenderness, such reverence.

"Happiest I've ever been in my life. If it was raining right now, I'd go dance in it."

And fuck, I would be right there by her side, getting drenched.

I gazed down at her, unable and unwilling to hide the awe climbing my face. Even now, a year later, her words never failed to ignite something in me. I'd wanted a love as deep and intense as my parents', despite all their faults, but I'd never been prepared for the depth of my feelings. They were endless, seamless. Scattered with stars.

Talia wiggled against me, a dance of pure delight, and I felt her happiness as strongly as if it were my own, surging through my veins. I couldn't keep it inside any more than she could.

I kissed the corner of her mouth and murmured, "Come with me."

Talia threw Ellie a hand to signal five minutes as I led her out of the room, down a corridor to a quiet terrace lined with Christmas lights and fake flickering candles. I shucked off my suit jacket first, draping it around Talia's shoulders before pulling her outside. It was milder than usual for mid-December but late enough for the evening chill.

"Oh, wow," Talia said softly. "This is beautiful."

I finally took my eyes off her. Big Ben and the Houses of Parliament were lit up across the river, a shimmering reflection on the water below. But none of it was as beautiful as the woman tucked by my side, swamped in my jacket, snuggling into the heat of my body still trapped inside the silk lining. The emerald of her earrings caught the candlelight on a nearby table, a glow that matched her eyes, and it was too much.

"I didn't want to do this tonight," I admitted, but I couldn't hold it in any longer.

"Do what?" Talia frowned. "What do you mean?"

"Do you remember that night, when I crowded you up close and fucked you against the wall until you came all over my hand?"

Her breath rang sharp in the air. "How could I forget? You want a repeat performance?" She glanced around the terrace and back again. "I'm game but it's a bit cold out here and not as dark as last time. Plus, I'm a respectable businesswoman now. If we're gonna do this, I need it to be more discreet. Like a coat closet or something."

I laughed, drawing her closer by the lapels of my jacket. "I always want a repeat performance and I will find the nearest closet possible, but right now, I want you to know... I need to tell you... Fuck. I don't know where to start."

She gazed up at me in that soft, blissful way of hers. So much love I almost couldn't handle it. I still wasn't used to all this adoration. Someone constantly looking at me like I hung the damn moon and all the stars. Did she know I felt the same way about her?

"Start at the end and work your way backwards," she suggested. "That always helps me."

I brushed my thumb across her lower lip as it curved with a smile. "Will you marry me?"

Talia's mouth dropped open. She couldn't seem to tear her eyes from my face, not even when I reached into my suit pocket, pulled out the jewellery box and flipped open the lid.

Diamonds and emeralds twinkled out from the black velvet setting; a perfect match to her dress, and I hadn't even planned it that way. Another reason it had to be tonight. It was like all the stars had aligned and I would have been an idiot to not notice.

"I've been carrying this ring around for months, waiting for the perfect moment, and it's been hard because the truth is, every moment with you feels perfect to me, no matter what we're doing."

"Rafe," she said on a breathy whisper, eyes glistening in the low light.

"And I promise you, I wasn't going to do this tonight because I didn't want to detract from your big night, making it about us. I want you to have your own special moments where we celebrate you and nothing else. But you said you were the happiest you'd ever been, and I had to do this now, Talia. I had to. Because I feel the same and I need you to know that. How happy you make me. How proud I am to be the one who stands by your side. I love you and I want to be your husband. I want you to be my wife."

Tears dotted Talia's cheeks and she blinked rapidly, sniffling as she smoothed them away with the back of one hand. "Yes," she croaked out through a smile. "Of course it's yes."

I huffed a laugh of utter relief. The tension tightening my shoulders slipped away with that one perfect word. "You sure? You ready for a life with a grumpy bastard like me?"

She stepped closer, nodding and sniffling all the while, and grabbed my tie, forest green to match her dress. I had a lifetime of colourful matching ties ahead of me and couldn't think of anything better. She gave the silk a gentle tug, drawing me down to her mouth, and her whispered words were the sweetest tasting sound.

"I thought you'd never ask."

THE END

WHAT'S NEXT?

What's next for Rafe and Talia? Sign up to my newsletter for an exclusive extended epilogue.

https://dl.bookfunnel.com/yp0afarefm

As a newsletter subscriber you can expect monthly updates on my upcoming works, exclusive sneak peeks, cover reveals and more!

DEAREST READER

Thank you so much for reading *One Week With You* and taking a chance on a new author. It means so much to me that you've chosen to spend your time reading my story.

I hope you enjoyed Rafe and Talia as much as I enjoyed writing them. These two took over my brain when I should've been working on my novel and I had no choice but to stop and listen!

If you can, please consider leaving a review on Amazon or Goodreads. I'm so grateful for your support either way. Indie authors couldn't do this without any of you so thank you.

If you're interested in my future works, my first full-length novel releases 2023. I'll be teasing more details about that over on my Instagram @jrjennerauthor very soon so I hope you'll join me there.

Eventually, Talia's brothers, Leo, Oliver and Jacob, will be getting love stories of their own but you might find them popping up in some other stories first. Rafe and Talia too. It's all interconnected so watch this space. There is so much more to come!

Until next time…

Love JR

ACKNOWLEDGMENTS

It feels surreal trying to write acknowledgements for a book I never thought would materialise. A long time ago I stopped writing for many years for many reasons—depression, self-doubts, the list goes on. So to be here now feels like a dream.

Thank you to my beta readers for the words of encouragement. I cherish the time you've spared for me. Amber, your words and compliments will stay with me and gave me the boost I needed to persevere when I considered giving up. Thank you.

To the ARC readers who not only took a chance on an unknown author, but also read a Christmas story in October. I'm so unbelievably grateful. I hope you'll take a chance on me again.

Aimee, my editor, who graciously allowed me to push back my original deadline and then did everything to make this November release work. Thank you so much.

Also, thank you to the online writing community. Reading posts about your own journeys helped me continue with mine. Writing is a lonely road more often than not and you all helped it be a little less so. I hope I can pay it forward someday.

Finally, thank you to my mum for always believing in my writing and reminding me of that belief often. You're not much of a reader so you probably won't read this but I needed those words more than you'll ever know. <3

ABOUT THE AUTHOR

JR Jenner lives in London, England. As a teenager, she first discovered romance through vintage Mills & Boon and has been hooked on the genre ever since. When she's not reading and writing, she loves shipping fictional TV couples, visiting the theatre and travelling when she gets the chance. Otherwise, dreaming of the next big trip is the next best thing.

One Week With You is her debut novella. Her first full-length novel is expected 2023. You can connect with her on the social media sites listed below.

- amazon.com/author/jrjenner
- bookbub.com/profile/jr-jenner
- facebook.com/jrjennerauthor
- goodreads.com/jr_jenner
- instagram.com/jrjennerauthor
- pinterest.com/jrjennerauthor
- twitter.com/jrjennerauthor

Printed in Great Britain
by Amazon